BEWARE!!
DO NOT READ THIS
BOOK FROM
BEGINNING TO END!

"Don't go in the basement!" your aunt warns as you start a game of hide-and-seek with your two horrible cousins.

Do you listen? No way!

But while you're hiding in the basement, your stomach grumbles and growls. You open an old refrigerator and find a jar of purple peanut butter and a stale chocolate cake. Which should you eat? Watch out: a SMALL taste of one of these foods could cause BIG trouble—you may never be the same again!

You're in control of this scary adventure. You decide what will happen. And how terrifying the scares will be.

Start on page 1. Then follow the instructions at the bottom of each page. You make the choices.

SO TAKE A LONG, DEEP BREATH, CROSS YOUR FINGERS, AND TURN TO PAGE 1 TO *GIVE YOURSELF GOOSEBUMPS*!

**READER BEWARE—
YOU CHOOSE THE SCARE!**

Look for more
GIVE YOURSELF GOOSEBUMPS adventures
from R.L. STINE

Give Yourself Goosebumps

Beware of the Purple Peanut Butter

R.L. Stine

Scholastic Children's Books,
Commonwealth House, 1–19 New Oxford Street,
London WC1A 1NU, UK
a division of Scholastic Ltd
London ~ New York ~ Toronto ~ Sydney ~ Auckland

First published in the USA by Scholastic Inc., 1996
First published in the UK by Scholastic Ltd, 1997

ISBN 0 590 19678 2

Typeset by Rowland Phototypesetting Ltd
Bury St Edmunds, Suffolk
Printed by Cox & Wyman Ltd, Reading, Berks.

10 9 8 7 6 5 4 3 2 1

You can't believe your parents have done this to you!

Your mum and dad are off to Europe on a business trip. So you have to spend the summer in Fiskeville with Aunt Fiona and Uncle Harvey. Which means spending the summer with your cousins Barney and Dora.

Which means a summer of torture.

Barney is a year older than you, and a bully. Dora is a year younger, and a whiny pest. Not what you had in mind for your summer holiday.

You stare glumly out of the car window as your aunt and uncle drive home from the airport. Aunt Fiona turns around in the front seat and beams at you. "Barney and Dora can't wait till we bring you home," she squeals.

I bet, you think. Bad-News Barney can't wait to pound me into the ground. Dora the Drag can't wait to rope me into playing with her dolls.

Uncle Harvey pulls the car into a driveway. You stare at the house. It's two storeys high and run-down. The lawn is choked with weeds. The front steps are cracked and crumbling. Not very promising.

At least the creepy cousins aren't around, you think. Maybe you can sneak off before they know you're here.

Then a loud *bang* makes you nearly jump out of your skin!

Go on to PAGE 2.

2

Barney runs out the front door, letting it slam behind him. You slowly step out of the car. Barney's pudgy face breaks into a mean grin under his thick blond hair. Even though he's only a year older than you, he's twice your size. While your aunt and uncle unload the car, he punches you on the arm, *hard*.

"Hi, wimp," he snarls.

Dora skips around the side of the house, holding her obnoxious orange cat, Puff. Dora's dark hair hangs in two long braids over her shoulders. She eyes you with a smirk, then giggles. Puff hisses at you.

What a summer! you think. Maybe you can spend the whole holiday upstairs in your room.

But no. "We've been waiting for you," Barney says. "Let's play hide-and-seek."

Oh, no, you think. It's starting.

"It's nice to see you're already having fun," Aunt Fiona gushes. "Your uncle and I have to go back to work at the university. I'll take your suitcase upstairs for you."

"No, really—" you protest. "I don't mind—"

"Nonsense," Uncle Harvey responds. "You kids go on and play. There's just one thing. It's very important. You can play anywhere you want, but don't go in the basement."

Turn to PAGE 23.

The water bug tries to climb on to the stick. You notice that it has wings. Which gives you an idea.

An idea that makes you want to puke.

You reach out and pat the water bug. Its body feels hard and slimy. It waves its antennae at you. It seems to like you.

Great. I've found a new friend, you think.

A friend who is so disgusting that now even Barney looks good!

You pat the huge brown bug again. Then you climb on to its back. It doesn't seem to mind. You grab hold of its antennae, and kick the bug in the sides as if you were riding a horse.

As you hoped, it spreads its wings.

The next moment, it's flying!

Up, up, up!

Fly on to PAGE 104.

You don't want to get in trouble on your very first day here. You take off running. You notice the other kids scattering in all directions. After you've put some distance between you and the field, you glance back. By the time the police car arrives at the baseball field, it is completely deserted.

Phew, you think, that was close.

Your rumbling stomach reminds you that you are still hungry. That chocolate cake wasn't enough. As you head for home, you realize that now even Uncle Harvey's shoes are too tight. Your toes are scrunched up inside the trainers. You walk by a neighbour's window and catch a glimpse of your reflection in the glass.

You can't believe your eyes!

You are at least thirty centimetres taller than you were this morning.

Turn to PAGE 134.

You run down the street to the left. The number 5 bus pulls up just as you arrive at the corner.

By now you're so small that you have to stand on tiptoe to drop your coins into the box. And when you arrive at the university, you can't reach the rope to signal for a stop. Luckily, some other people are getting out, too. You slip off the bus behind them.

The university is huge. Dozens of big red-brick buildings surround a grassy area. People hurry along the pathways.

How will you find your aunt?

A sign points to the main administration building. Maybe that's where you can find out where Aunt Fiona is. You head that way. Then those pink dots appear again. Thousands of dots.

When your fingers and toes stop tingling, you discover that you are now the same height as the dandelions on the lawn!

At the rate you're shrinking, you might disappear before you make it to the main building.

Should you run into the physics building right in front of you? Maybe one of the scientists will be able to help you.

Or should you keep going to the main building to find your aunt?

If you dash into the physics building, zoom over to PAGE 39.

If you keep looking for your aunt, turn to PAGE 126.

You want to try to talk to Barney. You watch him race for the house.

"Stop!" you shout. The sound of your voice makes the whole garden shake.

You pick Barney up in your hand. He screams in terror.

"No!" he yells. "No! Put me down! Please put me down!"

You've never seen him so scared before. You've never seen *anyone* so scared before. He really thinks you're a mutant alien!

"Please," he repeats, sobbing. "I'll do anything you say. Just don't hurt me."

Your face is too big for him to recognize. Barney has always been so nasty to you that you can't resist scaring him a little more.

You lift him even higher, until his toes dangle above the treetops. He kicks and screams even louder.

"Put me down!" he yells. "Please, please put me down!"

"Not yet!" you thunder. Then you bring him, squirming and crying, level with your face. "You puny human," you tell him. "I could smash you like a bug in a second. But I'll let you live on one condition."

Go on to PAGE 119.

You scoop her up in your palm and hold her close to your face while you explain what happened to you.

"I've seen cases like this before," she says when you finish. "I think I can help." She reaches into her robes and pulls out a small, torn brown bag.

"Take this herbal mixture," she instructs. "But take only a tiny part of it. The results can be very unpredictable."

You take the small bag from her hand and set her on the ground. "Thanks," you say. You're about to ask her more when she speaks again.

"Do as I say," she tells you. "Now, no more questions. It's time for my nap."

You blink once and she's gone. You almost think you imagined her. But the tiny brown bag sits in your hand.

You open it. A strong, spicy scent immediately fills the air. You shake the contents out in your hand. A small pinch of brown-and-green powder falls on to your palm. There's maybe a teaspoon altogether.

The fortune-teller told you to take a tiny amount of the mixture. But this *is* a tiny amount. And you're so big, you don't see how it can possibly help you.

Should you eat just part of the mixture? Turn to PAGE 79.

Or maybe you ought to take the whole thing—try PAGE 125.

You scurry into the nearby room.

It's a broom cupboard filled with cleaning supplies. Mops and brooms hang on the wall. A pail that seems as big as a car sits on a shelf above your head.

You hear the caretaker's heavy footsteps approaching.

"In there!" the woman screams. "I saw it go in there!"

"Don't worry," the caretaker's voice booms. "I'll take care of it." He enters the cupboard.

You jump up and down, waving your arms. "I'm a kid," you shout as loud as you can.

The fat caretaker bends down and squints at you. "Hey!" he exclaims. "You're not a mouse!"

You let out a huge sigh of relief. Finally! Someone who can help you!

The caretaker picks you up carefully by the collar and brings you close to his face. "I don't believe my eyes!" he sputters. "You're a—! You're a—"

You watch the caretaker's huge eyes roll up into his head. Seconds before he faints, he drops you to the ground. Too bad you don't have enough time to scramble out of the way.

SPLAT!

You've come to a very

FLAT END

You hurry over to Dr Abbott. You try shouting at him. But he doesn't hear your feeble, squeaky voice.

You try pulling on his trouser leg. But all he does is shake his leg, sending you flying under the table.

How can you make him notice you? Then you get a great idea. Moving carefully, you untie the shoelaces on both of his shoes. You're so small that it's like untying two skipping ropes.

Now, slowly, carefully, you tie the two laces together. You make a knot. He's so busy working he doesn't notice. You scramble out of the way and wait.

It doesn't take long.

Dr Abbott stands up. He starts to cross the room. *BAM!* He trips and falls flat on his face.

"Hey!" he shouts angrily. "Who tied my shoes together?"

"I did," you reply. He's still lying flat on the floor. You stroll over to his head.

"Who said that?" he demands angrily. "Speak up!"

"I did it," you repeat. You're standing in front of his face. "I'm sorry—I had to get you to notice me."

Now he focuses on you. At first he looks surprised. Then he frowns. He suddenly swoops his hand out to swat you.

Go on to PAGE 51.

You glance up to see a woman dressed in a silver bathing-suit. She's hanging upside down from a high wire. One end of the wire is caught in your hair!

"Hey!" she shouts at you. "Get out of my act!"

"I'm sorry—" you apologize. "I didn't mean to bother you." You reach up and untangle the wire from your hair. The crowd goes wild. They're applauding *you*. You smile at them and bow.

"Here comes the owner!" the tiger trainer declares. "You're in big trouble now!"

You peer down to see a small, fat man in a clown suit approaching. He has a white face with two huge black eyes and a bright pink nose.

"I'm sorry," you stammer, bending over to talk to him. "I didn't mean to ruin the circus. I only came here—"

"Ruin it?" the man cuts you off. "Are you kidding? This is the best act we've had in years! How did you get so big? How did you get the tigers to like you so much?"

"I can't really explain," you reply. "It all started—"

"Never mind!" the clown interrupts again. "I want to hire you! When can you start?"

Think quickly! The circus is a great place to hide out. But do you really want to spend the rest of your life here?

If you join the circus, turn to PAGE 113.
If you say no thanks, go to PAGE 118.

You dive for the can. Excellent! you think. You know what Monster Blood is from reading GOOSEBUMPS. Monster Blood makes things grow. Monster Blood will make *you* grow.

You hoist yourself on top of the floating can. You're sitting on top of the faded label. You brush some mud off and read: MONSTER BLOOD, SURPRISING MIRACLE SUBSTANCE.

Slowly, you crawl down the can to the lid. The can rocks back and forth in the murky water. You feel as if you're balancing on a log. The brown water laps over the sides of the can.

With all your strength, you tug at the lid. It's wedged tight. You tug and tug.

You have to get it open. You know the slimy green Monster Blood inside will make you grow.

You grit your teeth and give one final tug. The lid pops off and splashes into the water!

You reach your hand into the can and feel . . .

Go to PAGE 43.

You've got it! You'll find your aunt at the university. She can get you a doctor's appointment. Or maybe someone at the college will be able to help you. You race into the study. You search in your aunt's desk drawer for directions to the university.

Finally you find a bus map. There are two buses that seem to go to the university—the number 103 and the number 5. They leave from opposite ends of your block.

You don't know which bus is best. You don't want to wake up Barney and Dora to ask them. They've caused you enough trouble already.

You'll just have to guess.

Which bus will you take?

For the number 103 bus, race over to PAGE 103.

Or take the number 5 bus on PAGE 5.

You quickly spin on your heels and sprint towards the kitchen.

Barney lunges for you. Clumsily, he trips over his own feet and falls on the floor.

Without stopping, you yank open one of the lower cupboard doors and wriggle inside. You're so small now that you easily slip in among the pots and pans.

Barney will never find you here! You hear him stomping into the kitchen just as you pull the cupboard door shut.

"Where are you?" he demands. "You can't hide from me for ever!"

Wanna bet, you think.

You hear him open the door to the pantry, then slam it shut. Luckily, he never got a good look at you. He has no idea that you are now small enough to fit into this little cupboard.

"Wimp!" Barney hollers. "You'll have to come out sooner or later!"

Definitely later, you think.

You hear the TV click back on. From the sound of it, Barney's watching a really noisy racing-car programme. This will be a great time to leave the cupboard. There's no way he'll hear you climb out. Smiling, you prepare to climb out of the cupboard.

But then, a weird and familiar feeling comes over you.

What is it? Turn to PAGE 72.

14

Your problem is that you're hungry.

The plane ride to Fiskeville was a long one. All you had to eat was an airline snack of peanuts and a soft drink. And now you realize that you're starving.

Your stomach is growling so loudly you're almost afraid Barney and Dora will hear it.

You glance around the basement again. Maybe there are some cans of food.

But no. The only shelves contain old carpenter's tools. The only cabinets are full of torn and dirty sheets and towels.

You really don't want to go back upstairs. Not yet. Not with Barney the Bully and Drippy Dora waiting for you.

What about the old refrigerator? You see that it's plugged in. Maybe there's something to eat inside.

Trying not to get your hopes up too high, you approach the refrigerator. The door seems stuck. But you pull hard and it pops open.

You spot two containers right at the back. You bend down to inspect them. And gasp!

Turn to PAGE 29.

You peer up the stairs. The basement door leading to the kitchen is so small. Will you be able to fit through it?

You start up the stairs, hoping to make it to the top before you are too big to get through the door.

SMASH! Your foot crashes through the bottom step. They're just old and rickety, you tell yourself. You lift up your other foot and place it on the next step. *CRASH!*

The stairs won't work. You glance around the basement. You've got to get out before you're trapped inside. You have to move fast—you're still growing!

You notice a window. It will be a tight squeeze, but it's your only hope. You pull open the window. You're so big now you accidentally rip it out of its frame. Pieces of wood and glass fly everywhere. You start to climb through.

You don't really fit. But you're already half-way out. You refuse to give up now. You can hear the house ripping and tearing as you push your way through. Broken pipes spurt water. Torn wood scrapes your skin.

At last, you fall on to the lawn. You glance up to see a huge hole in the wall where the basement window used to be.

And then you hear a piercing scream.

Turn to PAGE 90.

16

At this size, you wouldn't be surprised if you could lift an elephant.

You'll give it a try. You bow to the cheering crowd. The elephant bows also.

"The Amazing Strongo!" the ringmaster cries. "The strongest human being in the world will now attempt to lift Dodo the elephant!"

You approach the elephant. You study her from all sides. Finally, you decide the best technique would be to bend your knees and wrap your arms around her lengthwise. The elephant drapes her trunk around your neck and tickles your ear. "Cut that out," you whisper. "Now hold still."

The elephant holds still. You begin to lift. The elephant is heavy—really heavy. You manage to lift Dodo thirty centimetres off the ground.

The crowd is cheering you on. The elephant grunts happily. Then suddenly someone in the audience shouts, "Alien! Alien! It's the alien!"

Go on to PAGE 91.

Cautiously, you stick a fingertip into the purple goop. It feels soft and gooey, like peanut butter.

You stick out your tongue and take a teeny-weeny taste.

Awesome flavour! It's purple and it's slimy, but this weird peanut-buttery goo tastes like a combination of every delicious dessert you've ever had in your life.

You lick the rest of the purple goop off your finger, then you stick your finger back in the jar. You can't believe how yummy it tastes. You wish the whole jar were full of the purple paste.

Unfortunately, there wasn't very much, and soon the jar is empty.

But you're not hungry any more. In fact, you feel great!

You shut the refrigerator door and flop back down on the armchair.

A moment later you hear a loud thump at the top of the stairs. You glance up. Your heart sinks when you see what's there.

Hurry to PAGE 94.

18

The porch is now enormous. It's gigantic—as big as an aeroplane hangar.

Or maybe it's the same size. Maybe you've shrunk even more. Your heart thunders in fright as you realize you might keep shrinking till there's nothing left of you.

A thick forest of grass lies between you and the porch steps. You glance up at a towering yellow tree, and realize it's not a tree at all—it's a dandelion!

You're as small as an insect!

Your hands tremble, and sweat pours down your face. You feel yourself beginning to panic. You take a deep breath. Then you sit on a leaf and force yourself to think calmly.

You still need to find the refrigerator. You have to get another look at the jar of purple peanut butter. That's the only way you can think of to figure out how to stop shrinking. And get back to your normal size.

Even though you're so tiny, you're not a quitter. Finding the refrigerator will just be a little more difficult, that's all.

Feeling better, you stand up and prepare to make the long trek to the house. And then you hear a loud hissing sound.

You glance up to see a pair of gigantic yellow eyes staring straight at you.

Turn to PAGE 110.

You race towards the screen door. It seems miles away.

Puff lands on the porch, then takes off after you.

Ahead of you, the door swings shut . . . then opens again. The wind is making it swing.

You're almost there . . . just a few more centimetres—

—a heavy paw crashes down on your back.

Oh, no!

You feel Puff's hot breath on your neck. In terror you glance up to see her sharp teeth approaching your face.

And then, suddenly, she lifts her paw. She's letting you go!

You scramble to your feet and run towards the door again. You're only about fifteen centimetres from it when *SMACK!* Puff pins you again with her paw.

Now you remember that she always plays with her prey before she kills it. Your only chance is to reach the door the next time she lets you go.

But can you make it? It depends on whether this is your lucky day.

Is today Monday, Wednesday, Thursday or Friday? If so, turn to PAGE 124.

Or is it Tuesday, Saturday or Sunday? Turn to PAGE 31.

You feel stranger and stranger.

"Speak, alien!" Dr Harlan cries.

But your mouth won't move. You glance down at Dr Harlan and watch as he begins to grow.

He grows bigger and bigger, faster and faster. The bakery and trees are also shooting up. Just watching them makes you even dizzier.

All at once you realize that they are not growing—instead, you are shrinking! You're finally returning to your normal size! Whatever caused you to grow is wearing off!

In less than a minute you're standing next to Dr Harlan's red van. All around you people are running and shouting. You can still hear the squeal of sirens. Dr Harlan is speechless. He seems frozen in shock.

Trying to appear casual, you stroll through the crowd.

"Hey, kid!" a policeman warns. "You'd better get out of here. There's a mutant alien on the loose."

"Really!" you reply innocently. Then you shrug. "Somehow that doesn't seem like such a big deal."

THE END

While you stir the mixture, Effy adds a tiny, tiny pinch of shrink powder. Then you close the dustbin lid and build a fire around it.

You wait while the cake cooks. It smells awful, but you don't care—you'll eat anything if it'll make you small again!

At last the fire dies down. When the dustbin is cool, you lift the lid and peek inside. The cake is green and lumpy. It smells like garbage mixed with too much cinnamon.

You can't wait to taste it.

You open your mouth wide and take a big bite. It tastes even worse than it smells. Your mouth feels as if it's full of slime!

But you chew it and swallow. Then you wait. Nothing happens.

"Eat some more," Effy suggests.

"It tastes too revolting," you complain.

Effy holds up two beakers of liquid—one purple and one blue. "Maybe one of these will help. A kid I know named Kermit gave these to me. Kermit's a really smart scientist."

You stare at the beakers and suddenly remember something. There was a kid named Kermit in a GOOSEBUMPS book you once read—*Monster Blood III*. And he invented a liquid that made things shrink. But what colour was the liquid?

Choose the blue liquid, turn to PAGE 67.
Pick the purple liquid, turn to PAGE 28.

There's no way you're going to play with bratty Dora and her dumb dolls. You cross your arms over your chest and glare at your cousin.

"Go ahead and tell," you taunt, "I don't care."

"You're going to be sorry!" Dora sneers at you. Then she disappears. You can hear her calling Barney.

Oh great, you think. I'm going to get pounded.

You can hear footsteps approaching. Your eyes dart around for a place to hide. You fling open the refrigerator and climb inside. The door swings shut behind you.

"No one's down here," Barney growls.

"But Barney, I tell you—" From your cramped hiding-place, you can tell Dora is bewildered. You hear them clamber back upstairs.

Fooled you! you gloat.

But the joke's on you. When you try to open the door, it won't budge! You throw all of your weight against it. Nothing! You realize you are stuck inside the refrigerator. And you are running out of air.

Frantically, you pound and shout. No one hears you. It will be hours before Uncle Harvey and Aunt Fiona come home from work. Barney and Dora are probably playing outside.

As you gasp your final breath you realize that even playing with Dora would have been better than this terrible

END

"Why can't we go in the basement?" you ask.

"We haven't cleaned it out since we moved in," Aunt Fiona tells you. "The people who owned the house before us were very strange. We don't know what's down there. It could be dangerous."

"Let's get started!" Barney commands when his parents have gone inside. "You remember the hide-and-seek rules?"

"I remember." You sigh. Who could forget?

"Whoever is *It* gets to pound anyone he catches," Barney reminds you.

"Fine," you say. "I'll go first."

"Sorry," Barney replies. "It's my house. I'll be *It* to start. Now go hide while I count to a hundred." He laughs as he waves his fist in your face. Then he shuts his eyes.

Gulp. Go on to PAGE 108.

24

You've decided to try to find the refrigerator. You need to get that jar. There may be a label on it that can tell you what to do! Or at least what the purple peanut butter is.

You race to the front door. You come to a sudden stop, slapping your hand to your forehead. You forgot—you don't know where the dump is. Or how to get there.

Great. Your only hope is Barney.

You'll be nice, you decide. Polite. You'll even beg. You search the house for Barney. You find him in the playroom, lying on the floor watching TV.

"Hi, Barney," you say sweetly.

"Mmmf," he grunts. He doesn't even glance at you.

"Barney—"

"Keep it down, will you?" he growls. He's watching *King Kong*. Probably identifying with the ape, you figure.

"Barney, please," you repeat. "I need to—"

"Would you shut up?" Barney snaps. His eyes are still glued to the screen.

Those weird pink dots are dancing in front of your eyes again. As soon as the tingling in your toes and fingers stops, you realize you've shrunk a few more centimetres. Now your head is level with the arm of the couch! When is the shrinking going to end? Are you going to shrink down to nothing?

Turn to PAGE 81.

You have an even number of letters in your first name. You continue to duel with the mouse, thrusting your pin at it. You duck while the mouse tries to claw and bite you.

The mouse pauses for breath. It's just the break you need. You jab at the mouse, scratching it on the foreleg.

With a squeak of pain, it turns to you again. It's really mad this time. It opens its mouth wide and snaps at you.

You rush to the other side of the cupboard, but the mouse follows. Your only hope is to try to escape through the mouse hole.

You dive for the hole. The mouse is right behind you. You feel your head go through. You see green grass beyond—and freedom! Now your shoulders squeeze through the hole—but then you become stuck. You can't go any further forward. You try to wriggle back out, but it's no use.

The mouse is right behind you. You can feel its hot breath on your legs.

If only you could shrink, just a little more!

Unfortunately, there won't be time.

Too bad—looks like you lost this duel to the mouse. If you can't smile about it, try saying, "Cheese."

THE END

You glare across the field at Barney. You aren't going to let him keep you from joining the game.

You're in luck—you won't have to fight him.

"Wait a minute, Barney," says a chubby kid with blond hair. "This new kid isn't a shrimp. Come on," he tells you. "You can be on our team." You stick your tongue out at Barney and join the other team. You just hope they don't hate you when they discover the terrible truth.

You're the strike-out champ.

"Come on, kid," the chubby boy says. "You're up."

You'll give it your best shot. You take the bat and step up to the plate. You gaze at the pitcher, a mean-looking red-haired girl. You grip the bat tightly and wait for the pitch.

"Strike one!" cries the umpire.

You can't strike out, you think. Not with Barney's beady eyes trained on you. You concentrate on your next swing.

The pitcher zooms a fastball at you.

Swing the bat on PAGE 135.

Your big, mean, obnoxious cousin is looming over you.

"Found you!" Barney exclaims. "Now I get to pound you!"

You leap to your feet, but it's too late. Barney grabs you by your T-shirt.

"Let me go!" you shout, but it's no use. Barney has always been the meanest bully you've ever known. For years you've dreamed of being able to beat *him* up.

"What's the matter, wimp?" Barney taunts. "Afraid of me?"

"No!" you exclaim. You wish you meant it.

Barney punches you on the shoulder. You know it will make things worse, but you punch back. To your surprise, Barney lets go of your T-shirt. He stumbles backwards a few steps.

"Ow!" he cries. "I didn't know you could hit that hard!"

Neither did you! This could come in handy. You give Barney a karate chop on the arm.

"Stop it!" he cries. He starts to run. You can't believe it! Barney is running away from *you*!

Maybe this visit will be different, you think.

You figure it's safe to go back to the house. Barney probably won't bug you any more. You take two steps and you hear a weird ripping sound. Then you trip and fall over!

What happened?

Turn to PAGE 80.

You grab the beaker of purple liquid and pour it on the cake. The liquid quickly seeps through the cake, turning it a weird lavender colour. You take a big bite.

Then you wait.

And wait. And wait.

Suddenly your teeth start to chatter. Your knees begin to knock. Your body sways back and forth.

It's working! you think. It's finally working.

Your teeth chatter faster and faster. You're afraid your fillings will fall out.

Then your body quietens down. You glance around. You've returned to normal size again!

"Hey, Effy!" you cry. "Look at me!"

You try to run over to Effy. But you can't. You can't bend your arms. Or your legs. What's going on? Your neck is incredibly stiff too.

"Oh, dear," Effy says. "I guess the purple liquid was the wrong one. You've been turned into a gingerbread man."

"What?" you cry, suddenly noticing your colourful icing clothes.

"Don't worry," Effy says. She leads you inside the bakery. "Gingerbread cookies are big sellers this year. I'll put you at the front and in the centre of the display. I'm sure I'll find a new home for you before you get too stale!"

THE END

Something in the refrigerator smells great! It smells so good, your mouth starts watering.

You were hungry before, but now you're ravenous.

Whatever is giving off the smell must be the best-tasting food in the world!

You pull out the two containers and examine them. One is a small jar. At the bottom of the jar is a blob of disgusting-looking purple goop. The other container is a white bakery box with a label that says EFFY'S BAKERY, MIDVALE in fancy writing.

Inside the box is a thick slab of chocolate cake.

You lean down and sniff. To your surprise, the delicious aroma is coming from the purple goop. It smells like a combination of the best peanut butter and jelly in the world, with chocolate on top.

The cake doesn't have any smell at all.

Your stomach growls again.

Which will you eat? The wonderful-smelling purple goop or the chocolate cake?

If you taste the purple goop, turn to PAGE 17.
If you try the cake, go on to PAGE 111.

You were born in one of the first six months of the year. You jump as hard as you can on to button number six.

For a moment nothing happens. Then the laser begins to buzz. You turn and stare as the machine glows green, then white, then yellow. You suddenly feel very sleepy. So sleepy that you have to take a nap.

When you awaken, you find yourself curled up on the lab table, wearing a white lab coat. You stretch and yawn. You feel strange. You feel *big*. You stand up and notice that you're much taller than you've ever been. You rush to the window and gaze into the glass.

Dr Abbott's face gazes back at you.

You glance at your hands. They're hairy adult hands.

Now you glance around the lab. With shock, you see a kid sleeping on a chair. The kid's eyes slowly open. There's something very familiar about this kid . . .

The kid is *you*!

Turn to PAGE 132.

Puff lifts her paw again.

You immediately wriggle free and rush towards the door.

Just as you reach the door, the wind blows it open even wider.

Oh, no! Puff will be able to follow you inside!

But you have no choice. You scoot through the opening.

Puff is right after you—but the wind shifts just in time.

The door slams shut in the cat's face.

"MEOOOWWWR!" she protests. She glares at you through the screen. She hisses in anger.

"Too bad, kitty," you tell her. "Better luck next time."

But it's not over yet. You still have to figure out how to get back to normal!

Turn to PAGE 58.

As fast as you can run, you head for Midvale. The police cars speed after you. To your left is the highway. To your right is the river.

You get an idea. You stop running and step *over* the river. The police cars all come to screeching stops. With squealing tyres, they make sharp turns and speed back towards the nearest bridge. You smile to yourself. You have plenty of time now.

Soon you approach Midvale. Quickly you scan the business district. There it is—Effy's Bakery, a small, grey wooden building.

The residents of Midvale scream and run when they see you. You don't care. All you care about is finding Effy. As you approach, delicious smells pour out of the tiny building.

Using your little finger, you gently tap on the door.

A plump, grey-haired lady comes to the door. You expect her to scream, but she doesn't. Her tiny head tips backwards as her eyes travel up, up, up, to meet yours.

"May I help you?" she asks.

"I hope so," you reply. You explain your problem. "I think your cake caused it," you finish.

"So *that's* what happened to the chocolate cake," she says.

Go on to PAGE 62.

You've decided to try the new reducing machine. Arnold leads you to a room full of equipment. He takes you to the largest machine.

"This is the Super-Duper-Reducer," he says.

The machine is so big it nearly touches the ceiling. It has levers and straps and weights. There is a bench with padding and a seat-belt. It looks like some kind of torture device from an old horror movie. Maybe this wasn't such a good idea.

But before you can change your mind, Arnold pushes you on to the bench. You lie on your back, looking up into the twisted metal of the device.

Arnold places your head in a big steel helmet. You can't see anything. Only your mouth is exposed so you can breathe. He puts straps around your head, your wrists, and your ankles. Then he turns the machine on.

With a loud whirring sound, the machine begins to shake. The straps pull your arms back and forth, making them flap like wings. Some kind of pulley system yanks your legs up and down, making you kick like you would if you were swimming. At the same time, the helmet makes your head vibrate.

After several minutes the whirring stops. Your legs and arms stop moving. Arnold removes the helmet and unstraps you.

Did it work? Are you smaller?

Flip to PAGE 96!

You race down to the basement and open the refrigerator. The empty cake box is still sitting next to the jar of purple goop. You examine the cake box but there is no list of ingredients, just the name of the bakery. Frustrated, you shove the box back on to the shelf. The purple-peanut-butter jar rattles.

Then you have a crazy thought. If the cake made you grow, could the peanut butter make you shrink? It worked for Alice in *Alice in Wonderland*. Some food made her big, some food made her small.

You might as well try. You grab the jar and take a big spoonful of the stuff and swallow it. It tastes AWFUL! It's like a combination of Brussels sprouts and liver. You force yourself to swallow all the goop in the jar. Will you shrink?

You feel an odd tingling sensation all over your body.

It's working! you think. *I'm getting smaller!*

But then something bumps your head. You glance up to see the ceiling—centimetres from your nose. What's going on?

The refrigerator is far below you. All the furniture looks as if it belongs in a doll's house. Somehow, you've grown another thirty centimetres. The purple goop didn't make you shrink after all! Instead, it made you grow even faster! You're so big now you might not even be able to get out of the basement!

Quick! Turn to PAGE 15.

You figure it's too early in your visit to get into trouble.

"All right, all right. Where's the doll's house?" you ask Dora.

"Out on the porch," your cousin answers. "Follow me."

You start to follow Dora up the stairs, when, suddenly, you have to stop!

The strangest sensation comes over you. Your toes and fingers tingle and little pink dots swim before your eyes.

"Come on!" Dora whines from the top of the stairs. "You *said* you'd play."

You shake your head and everything is back to normal again. That was weird, you think. Maybe you just stood up too fast.

Dora stamps her foot impatiently. "Do I have to set Barney on you?" she warns.

"I'm coming! I'm coming!" You bound up the stairs. You feel a little tired. Those stairs must be steeper than they look.

You follow Dora out to the porch and sit beside her in front of the doll's house. You have to admit, the doll's house is pretty cool. It's three storeys high and filled with miniature furniture. There's even a tiny piano and a little guitar.

You reach into the doll's house to move a chair. As you do, you notice Dora's eyes open wide in surprise.

Turn to PAGE 102.

It's Dr Abbott! A teeny-weeny Dr Abbott!

"Look what's happened!" Dr Abbott calls from the floor. "I used the wrong settings. Now *I'm* small, too!"

Great, you think. What now?

"Don't worry," Dr Abbott assures you. "I'll be able to return us both to normal size. We have to reverse the settings on the laser gun. But we need the remote. Where's the remote?"

You scan the laboratory for the remote. "I see it!" you cry. "It's on top of a glass beaker on the next lab table over."

"It must have been thrown out of my hand when the room started shaking," Dr Abbott tells you. "It will take both of us to change the settings."

"But how can we reach it?" you ask.

"I'll climb up the table leg," Dr Abbott says. "Do you think you can jump to the next table?"

The tables are only thirty centimetres apart. But that's a big distance to someone as tiny as you. You approach the edge of the table and glance down. The floor is a *long* way down. If you fall, you'll probably break every bone in your body.

Maybe, instead of jumping, you should climb down to the floor and then up the other table leg. What do you think?

___

If you decide to take the leap, turn to PAGE 57.

If you think you should climb down, turn to PAGE 115.

You steer towards the quiet pond. The water seems thicker and dirtier here. Your Popsicle-stick boat moves slower and slower.

You approach the large brown insects.

And now you see them up close.

They're slimy, huge water bugs! They have long, waving antennae and fierce-looking jaws. They're about four times bigger than you. Even if you were your normal size, these bugs would be huge!

"EEEEEWWWWW!" you cry. You can't help it. You've always found water bugs disgusting. And now here they are all around you. It's your worst nightmare.

The big brown bugs climb up the walls and on the ceiling of the sewer. They swim in the water alongside you. They make hideous clacking noises. They're everywhere.

Now one of the bugs swims closer to you. Its long, slimy antennae reach out towards the Popsicle stick. Its disgusting, hairy legs paddle through the water.

The bug's beady black eyes focus on you. And now it's—oh, no! It's trying to climb up on the Popsicle stick next to you!

GROSS!

Turn to PAGE 3—if you can stand it!

38

You quickly duck inside the big top. It's incredibly noisy. You hear clapping, laughing, and the roars of wild animals in the ring. Even though you're gigantic, no one notices you at first. They're too busy watching the circus.

In the centre ring, a man dressed in white is surrounded by five tigers. The tigers sit on colourful stands. The man is making them do tricks. While you watch, a tiger jumps through a flaming hoop.

The crowd applauds. The man in white makes the tiger bow. But then, instead of returning to its stand, the tiger rushes out of the ring.

And it is running straight towards you!

Quick! Hurry to PAGE 87.

You need help and you need it now!

You dash to the physics building. You scramble up the single step just as someone opens the door. Quickly you scamper inside. You stop a moment to catch your breath. Being tiny sure is tiring!

You scurry along a long hallway searching for someone who can help you. Men and women come and go all around you. But they don't look down at their feet, so they don't see you.

"Help!" you cry. "Can someone help me?"

A woman hears you and glances down. "AAAK!" she cries. "A mouse!"

"Where?" you squeak, glancing around. And then you realize that she means *you*. You're so little she thinks you're a mouse!

"Kill it!" the woman shouts. "Someone find the caretaker!"

You'd better get out of the hall—quickly! Two doors are standing open. The one at the far end of the hall is labelled DR ABBOTT'S LAB. Can you make it there before the caretaker comes? Maybe you'd better enter the unlabelled door right next to where you're standing.

Duck through the door that's closest on PAGE 8.

Or try for Dr Abbott's lab on PAGE 109.

You just aren't strong enough to lift the elephant.

You struggle and strain and huff and puff, but it's no use. The audience boos and the clowns throw water balloons at you. Even the elephant looks disgusted. You are chased out of the ring by a group of clowns driving a tiny car and throwing confetti.

But don't be too upset.

You still wind up working with your friend, the elephant. In fact, you are put in charge of one of the most important jobs at the circus. You are responsible for keeping the circus environment clean.

That's right! You and your shovel have come to the tail end of this tale.

No one ever said all of show business was glamorous. And you've made it into the Big Time in the Big Top!

So, you are now spending a lot of time at the elephant's

BACK END

You're so big now you take giant steps. It doesn't take you long to outdistance the police cars and helicopters.

But you're much too big to hide anywhere.

You're going to have to find help.

But where? The police think you're a mutant alien. Your relatives are afraid of you. Who could possibly help you?

You think back to when your troubles started. If only you hadn't eaten that piece of chocolate cake. That must have been what caused you to grow. You can't think of any other answer.

You have to find the person who made the cake. It's the only solution.

But who made the cake?

You close your eyes, trying to remember the name on the cake box. Was it Effy's Bakery, Midvale? Or was it Maddy's Bakery, Elmville?

If you remember, you know exactly where to go. If not, you'll have to guess.

Head for Effy's Bakery on PAGE 32.
Or search for Maddy's Bakery on PAGE 74.

"I surrender!" you say to Dr Harlan.

But you're so big that your voice sounds like the rumbling of thunder. No one can understand you.

"Surrender or we'll capture you!" Dr Harlan repeats. "One—"

"I surrender!" you repeat.

"Two!"

How can you make him understand that you're giving up? In desperation, you raise your hands high in the air.

Unfortunately, a helicopter was buzzing above you at just that moment. Your hand brushes against it, and the small chopper falls to the ground.

"It's attacking!" the scientist screams.

"Wait!" you cry. "It was an accident!" Your voice is so loud that the windows in all the police cars shatter.

"Hit the ground!" Dr Harlan ducks under the van. "It's after us all!"

"No!" you cry. You get down on your knees and try whispering. "You don't understand!" you say. The breath from your whisper blows over a tank.

"Go to Plan B!" Dr Harlan cries. What's Plan B? you wonder.

Find out on PAGE 75.

Nothing.

You lie on your stomach and peek your head into the opening of the can. You can't believe your eyes.

The can is empty!

No Monster Blood! No miracle substance. No nothing!

The can quickly fills with the brown slimy water. You hold on tight as the can starts to go down.

Down.

Down.

Well, sailor, it looks as if you've made the wrong choice. You are sunk!

THE END

You take a deep breath and dash for the doll's house.

Behind you, Puff pounces and lands on the porch. She immediately bounds after you.

You feel her hot breath on your neck as you pull open the front door to the doll's house. You throw yourself inside and slam the door.

"MEOWWWWR!" Puff screams in frustration.

You peek through one of the windows to see her glancing at you. She tries to stick her paw in through the window, but her paw is too big.

You glance around. It's a pretty nice doll's house, with comfortable furniture. Too bad the miniature TV doesn't work.

You explore the rest of the doll's house, but it's just more doll rooms. A doll family sits in the kitchen. But the refrigerator is fake, and so is the food.

You flop down on the blue-and-white striped sofa and glance through the window. Puff paces back and forth in front of the doll's house.

She knows you're inside. You don't dare leave as long as Puff is out there waiting for you.

Then you hear something that gives you hope.

Turn to PAGE 117.

"SQUEAK!" the mouse repeats. Then it jumps on you.

"Hey!" you cry. You find yourself buried under mouse fur. The mouse's snout is right in your face—and its breath is hot and sour. "Let me go!" you yell.

The mouse squeaks again, more quietly, and then it licks your face. Is it getting ready to eat me? you wonder.

No, it's washing your face. When it's done, it begins to wash the rest of your body. Then it picks you up in its warm, moist mouth. Its teeth hold you firmly, but don't hurt you.

The mouse carries you back through the mouse hole to a crawl space beneath the house. And now you see where it's going: a soft grey nest made out of fur, twigs and grass. Nestled in the nest are three small, grey baby mice. Each baby mouse is about the same size as you.

"No!" you cry. But the mouse doesn't listen. It gives you another lick. Then it drops you in the nest, next to its children.

It seems that the mouse has decided to adopt you.

But cheer up—things could be worse. You'll be warm here, and you'll have plenty to eat— as long as you like cheese and bread crumbs.

The toughest challenge will be learning to stay quiet as a mouse.

THE END

The warm feeling spreads through your whole body. Your muscles tingle and the ground starts shaking. You hear a low rumbling sound.

Now the tree branches begin to whip past your face.

You glance up to see that the trees are once again *over* your head. The growth formula has finally worn off! You're back to your normal size!

Unfortunately, your hands are still gripping Barney's shoulders. Barney's mouth and eyes are open wide. He looks as if he's in shock. But as soon as you let go, he glares at you. He is angrier and meaner-looking than you've ever seen him.

"YOU!" Barney shouts. "The alien was just shrimpy stupid you!"

You take a baby step backwards. "Uh, Barney . . ." you begin.

He doesn't let you finish.

"What was that about a promise, wimp?" he snarls.

"Uh . . . nothing," you reply, starting to back away faster.

"How's this for a promise, cuz," he sneers. "I promise to pound you!"

You're glad to be small again. But you wish the formula had lasted just a little bit longer. At least long enough to have escaped from Barney.

Oh, well. It looks like your chance to get even with Barney has come to an

END

Are you serious?

Are you really so wimpy you won't go into the basement?

Just because your aunt and uncle told you to stay out of it?

Just because it might be dangerous?

Get real!

Return to PAGE 108 to choose again.

You wait in terror for the lizard's tongue to scoop you up.

But nothing happens. After a moment, you cautiously open your eyes. A few centimetres away, the lizard is calmly munching on what remains of a grasshopper.

It wasn't after you after all! You glance around at this new part of the dump. Just beyond the lizard, leaning against a large boulder, is a big white refrigerator with no door. It looks just like the one your aunt had in the basement!

You race over to the refrigerator. Is this the right one? Is the purple-peanut-butter jar still inside?

You're much too little to see what's on the shelves. You'll have to climb in to find out. But how?

You search through the rubbish surrounding you and find an old piece of kite string. To you, the string is as thick as a rope. It gives you an idea. You discover a rusty safety pin. You tie the string to the safety pin.

Then you twirl the pin over your head. *Just like the rock climbers use*, you think. When the pin is spinning really fast, you throw it up towards the refrigerator shelves.

Did it catch?

Find out on PAGE 133.

You get an idea. An excellent idea. In *Alice in Wonderland*, some foods Alice ate made her grow big, other foods made her small. Could the peanut butter and the chocolate cake work the same way? Maybe that's why they were together in the refrigerator in the first place!

Besides, you've got nothing to lose.

You look inside the box. It's empty, except for one chocolate crumb and a tiny smear of icing.

You're not very big. Maybe it will be enough.

But which will you eat? The crumb or the icing?

Try the crumb on PAGE 97.
Or taste the icing on PAGE 107.

50

You run to the bathroom. The mirror is even higher than it was last night. You have to stand on a stool to peer into it.

It's true. You look the same, but you're definitely smaller. Getting dressed, you notice that none of your clean clothes fit. They're all much too big—except the jeans and T-shirt you wore yesterday. They're smaller, too. Whatever made you shrink also made *them* shrink. But what was it?

"Yesterday. Yesterday," you mutter. You pace around the room trying to remember everything you did in the last twenty-four hours. You're so freaked out, it's hard to concentrate.

"Okay," you say to yourself, trying to calm down. "I've been on aeroplanes before, and I've never shrunk. I've had my aunt's cooking before, so it's not what I ate for dinner . . ."

Suddenly, you snap your fingers!

You've figured it out! The purple peanut butter! You've never had anything like *that* before. In fact, you're not even sure what that purple goop was.

You'd better find out—and fast!

You race downstairs and straight to the basement. But when you yank open the basement door, your heart stops!

Go to PAGE 100.

You sprint out of Dr Abbott's reach. "Please don't hurt me," you beg. "I need your help."

"How can I hurt you?" he replies angrily. "You don't exist."

"What do you mean?" you demand.

"I've been working too hard," Dr Abbott mutters. "I'm starting to see things." He sits up and unties his laces, then reties his shoes. He rubs his eyes.

"I'm a real kid," you insist. "You're not imagining me. I'm really here."

He eyes you suspiciously. You try to look as real as possible. "I know!" you cry. "Ask my Aunt Fiona. She works right here at the university."

"You have references?" the scientist asks incredulously.

"Please! You have to believe me." Quickly, you explain what's happened to you. "I think it was the purple peanut butter I ate," you finish. "But whatever it was, I keep on shrinking. If you can't help me, I'm afraid I'll get so small I'll disappear."

Dr Abbott stares at you in silence. Then, suddenly, his mouth turns up in a big smile. "Kid," he says, "you've come to the right place!"

Turn to PAGE 86.

A Popsicle stick floats right up to you.

You climb on to it. At least you don't have to tread water any more.

But how will you get out of the sewer system?

You notice a toothpick floating by. You reach out and grab it. Using it as an oar, you begin to paddle your Popsicle-stick boat swiftly through the current.

After a few smelly minutes, you hear splashing ahead. The splashing sound grows into a roar. You glance up to see white water. The current is rushing into a waterfall!

Off to one side is a swirling pool. It looks safer than the waterfall. But the pool is swarming with large brown insects.

What a disgusting choice!

You might as well leave it to chance. Toss a coin three times. If it comes up heads or tails three times in a row, steer your Popsicle stick to PAGE 77.

If the coin comes up two heads and one tail, or two tails and one head, move on to PAGE 37.

You decide to just head straight home. It's been a long day. You don't need anything else exciting to happen to you!

On your way home, you pass by a pay phone.

CLANK! CHINK! CLINK! CLACK!

You find yourself covered in coins.

By the time you've reached your uncle's house, seventy-three dollars in change is stuck all over your body.

The extra money could come in handy, you think. If anyone asks where you got it, you'll say you just found some extra change in your pockets ... in your shirt ... in your socks ... on your elbow ... on your knees ...

THE END

54

It's a circus!

There will be people of all sizes at the circus, you figure. And the big top is large enough to cover you, and there are several smaller tents besides. You're sure you could fit inside any one of them.

You leave the highway and start running through a field. You frighten several horses and half a herd of cattle, but then you safely reach the circus grounds.

But you are still being hunted.

The police cars and helicopters aren't far behind. Quick! Which tent will you enter?

The big top? Turn to PAGE 38.
Or enter the sideshow tents on PAGE 130.

The lizard slithers out of the refrigerator. It's already as big as a Great Dane. It starts to follow you.

Terrified, you start to run. But it steps in front of you.

"Back!" you tell it. "Get back!"

You search frantically for something to use as a weapon. Just as you reach out to grab a rusty car door, the lizard stretches its head towards you. Its long tongue darts out.

But instead of trying to chomp you, it licks your hand. It wags its long, skinny tail. It isn't going to eat you. It likes you!

The lizard follows you all the way home. It's very friendly. You discover it really likes to play "fetch". You can't help noticing, though, that every time it comes back with the stick you've thrown, it has grown a little bigger.

By the time you reach your aunt and uncle's house, the lizard is the size of an elephant.

"Hey, wimp!" Barney calls from the porch. "Where have you been?" Suddenly, his eyes widen and his mouth drops open. He's just noticed your new pet dinosaur.

The lizard hisses at your cousin. You pat its scaly back. "Easy, boy," you say soothingly.

"Wha-what's that?" Barney stammers.

You smile at him sweetly. "Barney, meet my new bodyguard."

THE END

You gaze at the tigers. They gaze back at you. They look just like overgrown pussy-cats.

You reach down and scratch one of the tigers behind the ears. It arches its back and rubs against you, purring. The other four tigers jump off the platform and run up to you. All they want is to have someone treat them nicely.

"What are you doing?" Tombo screams. "You're ruining my tigers!"

You ignore him. You sit down on the dirt floor. The tigers all crawl into your lap. You pet them. They lick your hands and face. The crowd loves it. They cheer even louder than they did for Tombo.

"You see, Tombo?" you say cheerfully. "You should be kinder to your tigers."

You're having a great time. You're even going to get paid. What a life!

In fact, everything is *purr*-fect until your hands and feet start to feel warm. The feeling moves up your arms and legs. Soon your whole body feels as if it's on fire.

What's going on? you wonder.

You're not on fire—you're shrinking! What a time to grow small again!

Just when you have five tigers on your lap!

THE END

How can I make that jump? you wonder.

You gaze around, desperately. And then you spot something that might help. A pencil. It's twice as tall as you are—just the right size for a vaulting pole.

You've never vaulted before. But you've seen athletes do it on television. You grasp the pencil, point side up. Then you take off running towards the edge of the table.

Please let this work, you pray. Just before you reach the edge, you jam the eraser end of the pencil down on the table. Then you leap.

You sail through the air. You don't look down.

Hooray! You land on the other table! A moment later Dr Abbott scrambles up beside you.

"The remote's over there," you tell him, pointing. The remote is balanced across the top of an open glass jar.

The two of you make your way across the table. Dr Abbott is a very messy worker. The table is covered with junk. You have to detour around dirty coffee cups. You scoot around piles of books. You've almost reached the jar when you trip over a big paper clip.

At last you reach the glass jar. The remote sits on top of it, far beyond your reach. Was it all for nothing?

Turn to PAGE 92.

58

Somehow, you have to get to the dump and find the refrigerator. It's your only hope. But how will you do it? It would take you weeks to walk. And you can't call a taxi—even if you could reach the phone, you're too small to dial.

There's only one answer. Somehow you must get help from your dear, disgusting cousins.

You head for the living room. Dora and Barney are sprawled on the floor, watching television.

"Dora! Barney!" you yell as loud as you can.

But it's no use. Your voice is too feeble to be heard.

You approach Dora and tug on her shoe. She doesn't even notice. She yawns and gets up. "This is boring," she announces. You're still holding on to her shoelace when she begins walking. You grab on tighter to keep from getting squashed.

She stops in the bathroom, and stands in front of the mirror. You glance up to see her reach into the medicine cabinet. She pulls out a small box.

You get an idea.

Turn to PAGE 122.

You roll yourself into a ball and brace yourself for a hard landing. But you're so small now, and so light, that you float like a feather.

The next thing you know, you're standing in a dense jungle of grass. You notice disgusting smells—rotting food, mouldy furniture, mildew and decay. But you don't care. Somewhere out there is the refrigerator with the solution to your problem.

All you have to do is find it.

You begin trudging through the tall, tall grass. You reach the top of a hill. On one side of the hill is a gigantic pile of twisted metal forms. They appear in all different colours: blue, red, green, yellow. Many of them are covered with rust.

On the other side of the hill is a thick jungle of vines and weeds. You can't see what might be dumped among them.

You're trying to decide which way to go when you hear a strange, loud noise. It sounds like a *HISSSSS!*

You glance around, then gasp in shock.

Approaching you through the grass is . . . a dinosaur!

Rush to PAGE 128.

You head for the jungle of weeds. The lizard runs after you.

It's hard to move quickly through the thick, tall grass, but you're desperate. You pass piles of rubbish, broken appliances, black, rotting mounds of ooze. You detour around slimy pools bubbling with the scent of rotting food.

Then your feet slip out from under you on a pile of slick, yellow mould. You tumble down a slope, unable to break your fall. You stop rolling at the bottom of the hill. You glance up to find the lizard staring down at you. It opens its mouth wide. Its mouth is so big you know it could swallow you in one bite.

Then it flicks its tongue out, straight towards you.

You close your eyes.

Are you about to be lizard lunch?

Find out on PAGE 48.

Arnold's could be just what you need. You *are* getting too big, and your clothes *do* seem to be shrinking. You ask the bus driver for directions.

A few minutes later you find yourself in front of a sleek low building. ARNOLD'S REDUCING SPA is spelled out in neon.

Hmmmm, you think, not exactly what you had in mind. But you might as well give it a shot. Especially since you realize that you've grown another fifteen centimetres on the way over.

You wonder why you don't feel anything—no tingling, no aching, no dizziness—when you grow. You have no way of knowing when it's happening. You hurry through the glass doors. A muscular blond man approaches you. "Hello," he greets you. "I'm Arnold. What can we do for you?"

"I'm getting too big," you explain. "Can you help?"

Arnold flexes a muscle and then beams. "Of course we can help," he tells you. "At Arnold's we pride ourselves on returning our customers to their original sizes. And we are offering a free one-day trial membership."

This sounds promising.

"You might try the steam room. Many members have found it helped them lose weight," Arnold suggests. "Or our new reducing machine. We haven't tried it yet—you could be the first."

Try the new reducing machine on PAGE 33.
Or go to the steam room on PAGE 105.

"What do you mean?" you ask.

"It was a special cake I made for a client who was too short. But another customer picked it up by mistake. When I called her, I found out she had moved."

Now you know how the cake ended up in your uncle's basement. "Well, it worked," you tell her sadly. "It worked too well."

Effy looks you up and down and then nods. "I must have put too much growth spice in it," she tells you.

"Is there any way you can reverse it? Can you bake a cake that will make me small again?" you ask.

Effy thinks, frowning. "I'll try," she agrees. "But it'll have to be a huge cake. You'll have to help me."

Gladly, you agree to help. First, Effy leads you to a huge dustbin behind her bakery. "Here's where I get rid of my mistakes," she tells you. The dustbin is full of mouldy, strangely-shaped cakes.

After you've cleaned out the dustbin, Effy brings fifty bags of flour and spices. You empty them into the dustbin. She climbs on a ladder and breaks a hundred eggs into the flour. Then she adds seven gallons of water from a garden hose.

"And now," she says, "for the shrinking powder . . ."

Turn to PAGE 21.

With a whine, the magnetron stops vibrating. You try to sit up. Then you notice that the gigantic metal tube has shrunk.

Suddenly, it fits snugly all around your body!

"Congratulations," Dr Abbott tells you. "It worked!"

Now you realize that the tube didn't shrink— you grew! You're back to your normal size!

You're also stuck in the tube. Dr Abbott fiddles with some controls on the magnetron. The two sides of the tube pop apart so you can climb out. But you notice something odd.

"My skin is sticking to the metal," you tell the scientist.

Dr Abbott frowns. "Don't worry about it," he says. "That's just a side-effect of the treatment."

You thank the scientist for his help. Dr Abbott smiles and walks you to the front of the physics building. "We'll be in touch," he tells you. "I'll need to write this up for the scientific community." As you're about to step outside, he stops you.

"My keys!" he exclaims. "You're walking off with my keys."

You glance down and notice a ring of keys plastered to your jeans. You pluck them off and hand them to him.

Strange, you think. But what happens next is even stranger.

Go to PAGE 66.

The growling turns to a nasty snarl. You feel a stinging on your ankle. You glance down to see the neighbour's dog, a rottweiler, attacking you. You're so huge it's like being attacked by a cricket.

You ignore the dog. You find more pieces of the roof and try to place them on the house.

There are still pieces missing, but it doesn't look so bad now. You dust your hands off and stand up. But now you hear a new sound behind you.

You turn around to see dozens of people approaching. They're holding golf clubs, kitchen knives, brooms and shovels. They look frightened but determined.

Not good.

"Hi," you say, trying to sound friendly. "I'm sorry I wrecked your roof. It's almost as good as new now."

The man whose roof you damaged shakes his fist at you. He holds a dustbin lid like a shield. "This is the alien!" he yells to the others, pointing at you. "That's the alien that destroyed my house!"

The others shriek and shake their weapons at you. "Get out of here, alien!" they shout. "Get out and don't come back!"

Maybe that's not such a bad idea. You're not sure where to go. But you're definitely not welcome here.

Escape on PAGE 106.

Then Dora's smile twists into a horrible grimace.

"Alien!" she shrieks. "The mutant alien!" The people in the front rows scream. They climb over their seats to get away from you.

"Dora, I'm your cousin!" you shout. You try to wriggle out of the powerful grasp of the elephant's trunk. But Dodo's clutching you too tightly.

"How could you be my cousin?" Dora is sobbing. "No! No! You're an alien!"

The crowd frightens Dodo the elephant. Dodo drops you. Right on top of a candy-floss machine. You are covered with the sticky pink stuff.

It's no use. No one will listen to you. You duck out of the tent and take off running.

I can cover more ground than anyone else, you reassure yourself. I'll be far away from that angry mob in no time.

And then you hear the sirens.

Go on to PAGE 121.

You reach the bus stop just as the bus for home pulls up. You try to drop a coin in the slot, but it sticks to your hand. The bus driver has to pull it away from your skin.

You have a growing suspicion that you know what the side-effect of the magnetron treatment might be. When you find yourself stuck to the metal seat at your stop, you're sure.

The magnetron restored you to your normal size, all right. But it also changed your magnetic field. Somehow, it's turned you into a human magnet!

Metal is now attracted to you. As you stroll home from the bus stop, metal objects jump off the pavement on to your legs. Parking meters and lampposts bend in your direction as you walk by. They look as if they are bowing.

This is pretty cool, you think. You turn to face a bent-over lamppost. "I am the Great Magnetron!" you announce in a grand voice. "Ruler of all I see!"

You could have some fun with this.

Do you head straight home? Then turn to PAGE 53.

Or if you want to see what other magnetic possibilities you have, go to PAGE 131.

You break off a piece of cake and dunk it in the blue liquid. You're sure Kermit used blue liquid to make things shrink in *Monster Blood III*.

You take a bite of the cake. Please work, you think, please—

And then, suddenly, you feel as if you're falling.

You gasp and glance around—you *are* falling!

You've suddenly become small again—all at once. And you're falling, straight towards the open dustbin.

SQUOOOOOSH!

You land right in the middle of the smelly, soft, slimy, disgusting cake. But you don't care. You climb out of the dustbin and thank Effy.

"You're very welcome," she replies. She hands you a towel. While you're wiping yourself off, she ducks inside the bakery. She returns with a big box of chocolate cupcakes. "Here you are," she says. "A treat to take home to your aunt and uncle."

"Thank you," you reply. You take the box and start home.

But as soon as you're out of sight you throw it away. You didn't want to hurt Effy's feelings—but you're sick of chocolate cake!

The next time you're hungry, you decide, it's Brussels sprouts and broccoli for you!

THE END

68

You were born in the last half of the year. You leap on to the remote. With all your weight, you land on button six.

The laser gun explodes with a loud *BANG!* Pieces of glass and metal rain all over the laboratory. In terror, you dive under a magazine. When pieces of the laser gun stop falling, you crawl out.

You're still tiny. It didn't work.

Dr Abbott is upset. "I can't believe it!" he mutters. "I was *sure* those were the right settings." You've decided that Dr Abbott is the stupidest scientist you've ever met.

"I have another idea," he tells you. "I'm *sure* this one will work."

"Thanks anyway," you tell him. You're *sure* you'll be safer finding help somewhere else.

"Don't leave me," the scientist begs.

You climb down the table leg. "I'll come back when I'm the right size," you assure him. "Maybe *I'll* be able to help *you*."

You hurry out of the lab. You overhear a student telling someone her address. She will be going right past your uncle's house. You sneak into her rucksack and hitch a ride.

You can't think of anything else to do but try to track down that jar of purple peanut butter.

Turn to PAGE 58.

Nailed on the door of Maddy's Bakery is a big sign that says OUT OF BUSINESS.

Sadly, you stand up. Maddy's was your only hope.

Now you notice that the noise around you has grown louder. Much louder. You glance around in horror.

In front of you are a dozen police cars.

Behind you are three tanks and an armoured personnel carrier from the National Guard.

Behind *them* is a big red van you've never seen before. On its side is painted ALIEN RESEARCH INSTITUTE.

Overhead small planes and helicopters buzz.

You hear a loud *SQUAWK!* and then a loud-speaker comes on.

"We've got you surrounded, alien!" a hollow voice cries.

"I'm not an alien!" you cry. "I'm a human kid!"

Now the red van opens. A skinny man with thick glasses steps out. "I'm Dr Harlan from the Alien Research Institute," he shouts through a megaphone. "I'm here to take you to our museum for study."

"I don't want to be studied!" you reply.

"Too bad," he says. "You'll never get away. Surrender now—or we'll be forced to capture you!"

Will you give up? Surrender on PAGE 42.
Or try to get away on PAGE 123.

Dora turns her head back and forth, admiring her reflection. You'd hate to be the one to tell her that she looks like a clown. You climb into the make-up box and wait. After a moment she reaches for an eye pencil. You grab on to the pencil. She'll *have* to pay attention to you now.

She picks up the pencil, then stops.

"AAACCCKKK!" she screams. "A gigantic, ugly bug!"

Before you can protest that you're not a bug, she shakes you off the pencil. You drop into the sink.

"Dora!" you cry.

But it's too late.

She's turned on the water.

The ice-cold water hits you. Like a waterfall, it pushes you down. You struggle against it, trying to breathe. You try to swim, but the current is too strong. And then you begin to spin, faster and faster.

You feel yourself being pulled down, down . . .

You open your eyes and see a huge silver circle approaching.

It's the plug-hole.

You're about to be swept down the plug-hole!

Go to PAGE 85.

You glance around quickly to make sure no one is watching. Then you push open the basement door and start down.

The stairs are old. They creak with every step you take. Cobwebs brush your face.

What could be down here that's so dangerous? you wonder.

You reach the bottom of the stairs. The floor is so dusty it looks as if it hasn't been cleaned in a hundred years.

Feeble daylight filters through a big, filthy window at the back of the room.

You start to explore.

But there's nothing much to see. Mostly old, dusty, worn furniture. Old couches, old chairs, an old mattress. An old refrigerator and stove, both covered with rust, sit in one corner.

Nothing dangerous. Nothing even interesting. But being down here is better than getting pounded by Barney.

You sit in one of the old armchairs and wait. Sooner or later Barney and Dora will get tired of their game. Soon it will be safe to go back upstairs.

There's only one problem.

A *big* problem.

Turn to PAGE 14.

Those annoying pink dots! That creepy tingling in your fingers and toes.

You're still shrinking.

Now, when you try to open the cupboard door you find it's much too heavy for you. You're not sure how small you've become, but the pots and pans now seem as big as cars.

What can you do? If you don't leave the cupboard you'll never be able to find the refrigerator and return to your true size. At this rate, you will have shrunk down to nothing before lunch!

"Help!" you squeak. "Help!"

Even if you were your normal size, you realize, no one would be able to hear you with all the racket coming from the TV.

Luckily, it's not totally dark in the cupboard. But why not? You glance around. You notice something you hadn't seen before. In the back of the cupboard you spot a small hole. Pale light is streaming in through it.

Maybe you can escape through the hole!

You crawl over a pile of pan lids towards the hole. You've almost reached it when you hear a hideous scratching sound. A moment later a huge, furry head begins to push through the hole. Yikes! What is it?

Turn to PAGE 127.

You've decided to tell the police what happened.

The police car pulls up. Two blue-uniformed officers climb out. "We're here about the broken window," the taller one says. "Did any of you kids see who did it?"

The other kids look down at the ground. The red-haired pitcher scuffs her foot in the dirt.

"I did it," you announce, stepping forward. "But it was an accident. It was my very first home run." The officer studies you for a minute. "How old are you, kid?" she asks.

You tell her and she looks surprised. "You're awfully big for your age," she says. "You'd better be careful. You don't know your own strength."

"I'll be careful from now on, officer," you promise.

"We'll let you go this time," she says, getting into the car. "Since it was your first homer." She winks at you.

What a relief! You watch the patrol car drive off.

"Come by and play tomorrow," the red-haired pitcher calls after you as the game breaks up.

You return to your relatives' house, and you notice something very strange. The porch roof is at least five centimetres closer to your head than it was when you left.

Is this *really* only a growth spurt? you wonder.

Go on to PAGE 95.

74

You run along the central reserve of the highway, heading for Maddy's Bakery. On either side, you hear the crashing of cars as drivers gawk at you. At last you see a big green highway sign: ELMVILLE, 23 MILES.

Twenty-three miles is no problem for you. It shouldn't take more than ten minutes or so.

With police and army cars speeding after you, you follow the highway. At last you see a sign for Elmville. By now the helicopters have caught up with you again. You wave your arms at them, swatting them away as if they were mosquitoes. If only they would leave you alone!

You turn towards the town, and quickly scan its tiny buildings till at last you find one that says "Maddy's Bakery".

Maddy's is a tiny brick building with a brown shingled roof. You kneel in the car park, and bend your head so you can see the bakery more clearly.

But what you see causes your heart to sink into your toes.

Turn to PAGE 69.

Plan B begins. The police cars and tanks suddenly back away. The roof of the red van peels back. Some sort of bizarre weapon pokes out from its roof.

"This is your last chance, alien!" Dr Harlan shouts. "Will you give up peacefully?"

"I'm not an alien!" you explain. "I'm a kid!"

"Your time is up!" Dr Harlan shouts. "Activate the web gun."

They're going to shoot you! Help! You turn to run.

BOOM!

Something heavy falls over your head. You try to pull it off, but thick strands pin your hands to your sides. The more you struggle, the tighter the strands wind around you.

In horror, you realize that the gun shot a big net all around you. Now the strands wind around your feet. You feel yourself start to topple to the ground.

"Congratulations, alien!" Dr Harlan's voice cries. "You're the first creature to be captured by our artificial spider's web!"

Somehow, you don't feel honoured.

Oh, well. That's what happens when you become too wrapped up in adventure.

THE END

"I'd like to try the magnetism," you tell Dr Abbott.

"Excellent," he replies. "I think you have a good chance for success. There's only one drawback . . ."

"What is it?" you ask anxiously.

"Never mind," he says briskly. "Compared to your present problem, it's minor." He wheels over one of the big machines from the corner of his lab. A label on its side reads SUPERMAG-NETRON.

The machine is as tall as Dr Abbott. It's covered with dials and buttons. A long tube as wide as a person runs right through the centre of the machine.

Dr Abbott picks you up and gently places you in the centre of the tube. You feel very tiny inside the huge machine.

"Hold very still," he instructs you. "No matter what you hear or feel, don't move!"

You hear a metallic *click*, and then a loud buzzing noise. The tube begins to vibrate, faster and faster. You try to hold still, but it's like trying to stay still during an earthquake. The buzzing grows even louder.

It's so loud you can't hear anything else. Your eardrums feel as if they're going to burst! And then, everything stops.

Did it work? Turn to PAGE 63.

The coin came up the same way three times. You guide your boat straight towards the waterfall.

How horrible could a waterfall in a sewer be, anyway?

You soon find out. Your Popsicle stick is sucked into the white water. You hold on as tightly as you can. *SPLASH!*

You're forced over the waterfall and into a long, wide pipe. You grip the Popsicle stick with your arms and legs. You tumble end over end through the dirty, rushing water.

You choke as water rushes into your nose and mouth. Just when you're about to drown, you reach the end of the pipe.

You climb back on top of your Popsicle boat. The swift current is now rushing you towards a big machine. The machine makes hideous grinding noises.

And then you realize what the waterfall was.

It was the main pipe for the sewage treatment plant!

You and the Popsicle stick are about to be ground into tiny pieces!

Up ahead you see the sharp metal teeth of the grinder.

GRRRRRRR! GRRRRRRR!

There's no way back. Only forward.

Too bad—this adventure is grinding to an

END

There's got to be a logical explanation. Maybe you didn't notice how much Dora has grown. Maybe you're losing weight. Maybe you're just imagining things.

"You're looking awfully thin, dear," Aunt Fiona tells you at supper that night. "Have some more mashed potatoes."

"Yeah, wimp." Barney grins. "Eat some of my food while you're at it." When his mother isn't looking, he dumps his broccoli on your plate.

You ignore Barney. Because you've just noticed something disturbing. The table seems a lot higher than it used to be.

Something really bizarre is happening to you.

I'll feel better after a good night's sleep, you think.

That night you have weird dreams about pink dots and tingling toes. And the next morning, when you climb out of bed, your pyjama bottoms fall off your body on to the floor!

What is happening? you wonder in a panic.

You pick up your pyjama bottoms and examine them. They are exactly the same as they were last night.

Of course they are. Because you now know what the problem is.

Your pyjamas haven't got bigger. Dora hasn't grown and your watchband hasn't stretched.

You have shrunk.

Turn to PAGE 50.

You stick out your tongue and lick up the teeniest, tiniest bit of the herbal powder. It's such a small amount, you don't even taste anything as you swallow.

You hold your breath, waiting for something to happen.

But nothing does.

"Notice any difference?" you shout down to the clown.

"No." He shakes his head. "But at least you aren't growing any bigger. Maybe you have to wait for it to work."

"Maybe," you agree. But you can't help being disappointed. Maybe you should eat the rest of the mixture. You start to lift your hand to your lips when you suddenly hear a familiar noise—

Sirens and helicopters!

Oh, no! The police have found you!

Should you eat the rest of the mixture?

Before you can decide, a helicopter swoops down outside the tent. Its rotors blow the rest of the mixture out of your hand.

The herbs are lost for ever on the wind.

You duck out of the big top and start running. You have to get away!

Run to PAGE 41.

You sit up and glance down at your feet. No wonder you tripped over. Your toes have burst through the front of your trainers!

You yank off what's left of the trainers. You wiggle your squished toes. You've heard of outgrowing shoes. But you never knew it could happen so fast!

You hurry into the house to find new shoes. You pass through the kitchen, where your aunt is packing her briefcase for work. "Why are you barefoot?" she asks.

"I think my shoes have shrunk," you answer. You show her the ripped trainers.

"Perhaps you're just having a growth spurt," she offers. "You look a little taller."

Up in your room, you study yourself in the mirror. You do look bigger. Maybe even a couple of centimetres taller than you were yesterday.

Your shoes are all too short. You have to borrow an old stinky pair of Uncle Harvey's trainers. They are a little too big for you, but they are comfortable. You're just tying the shoelaces when Dora sticks her head inside the room.

"I saw you in the basement," she announces. "And I'm telling!"

Turn to PAGE 129.

You have to get to the dump and you have to get there NOW!

Barney is your only hope.

"Please, Barney, I have to—"

"What part of 'shut up' don't you understand?" Barney demands. "I'm trying to watch TV! Do I have to teach you a lesson?" As he pulls himself up off the floor you realize you're so little now, he towers over you.

Maybe this was a bad idea.

"Uh . . . I'll see you later," you say and start to back out of the room.

But Barney means business. You've seen that nasty expression on his face before. It means he's really mad. And when Barney is mad— watch out!

Quick! Where can you hide from your cousin?

Dash into the kitchen and hide in a cupboard on PAGE 13.

Or find a hiding-spot outdoors. Run to PAGE 93.

"Get ready for another crummy tea party," the voice says.

You glance around, your heart pounding. "Who said that?"

"I did," the father doll replies. Its painted mouth doesn't move. But the voice is definitely coming from the doll.

"You can talk?" you exclaim.

"Of course I can talk," he replies. "So can you. All dolls can talk."

"I'm not a doll," you protest.

"Then what are you doing in our doll's house?" He walks towards you stiffly. "Are you a burglar?"

"No, no," you say. He may be a doll, but he looks strong.

"Of course you aren't," says the mother doll. "You're my new housekeeping doll." She brings you a tiny vacuum cleaner.

"But—" you start to protest. The mother doll glares at you. You shrug and start to vacuum.

"The new doll is dangerous and needs to be locked up," the father doll insists.

"No! There's too much work to be done. There's cat hair everywhere," the mother doll tells him.

You glance out of the window. Puff's yellow eyes glare back at you.

Will Dora ever come back? you wonder as you vacuum the rug. With all the cleaning you have ahead of you, a little tea would sure hit the spot!

THE END

You've got to stop Barney. You are now so big you're afraid if you grab him, you'll squash him. You have to act quickly—he's almost at the door.

You reach out and grab the first thing your hand touches. Unfortunately, it's the roof of the neighbour's house.

With a hideous *CRACK!* the roof rips loose from the house. Bricks and roofing shingles scatter like falling leaves. You've opened the house up like a box. You stare at the roof in your hand. Shocked, you peer into the house.

From inside, the neighbours stare up at *you*. They were eating lunch. Now they're screaming in terror.

"It's a monster!" the father of the family shouts.

"It's an alien!" his wife screams.

"Alien! Alien!" his daughters shriek.

"No—wait!" you cry. But your voice is so loud what's left of their house shakes. The family rushes out to the street.

You search for Barney, but he's disappeared. He's probably gone for the police. You feel terrible. Maybe you can fix the damage you've caused. You kneel down beside the house and carefully set the roof back in place. Unfortunately, parts of it seem to be missing. You glance around the garden for the missing pieces.

Then you hear an angry growl.

Turn to PAGE 64.

You find yourself eye-to-eye with another strange circus performer. Only this time it isn't a clown. This time it is an elephant!

"Hi, there," you say to the giant beast. You are so big now, you and the elephant are the same height.

The elephant gazes steadily at you. It seems to be waiting for you to do something. But what? You glance around. You realize you are at the back entrance to the big top.

Suddenly a voice booms over the loud-speakers. "Ladies and gentlemen! Children of all ages! You are about to be astonished by the extraordinary feats of The Amazing Strongo!"

The elephant looks at you expectantly. You have a funny feeling *you* are The Amazing Strongo.

The announcement continues. "Watch The Amazing Strongo lift an elephant into the air!"

You stumble through the flap. The elephant pushes you with its trunk! Then it nudges you all the way into the centre ring. You are surrounded by cheering people. When the applause dies down, the tent grows eerily silent. They are all waiting for you to go into your Amazing Strongo act. But you can't lift an elephant! Or can you?

If you are able to do five press-ups, turn to PAGE 16.

If you can do less than five press-ups, turn to PAGE 40.

The water forces you down the drainpipe. You try to swim, but the current is too strong. You hold your breath as you swirl underwater. Just when you think your lungs are going to burst, you splash into a deep, dark pool.

You push your head above water. You suck in a deep breath of air. A big wave pushes you back under. The next thing you know, your body is whooshing along a long, curving pipe.

The water slows slightly and you come up for air. Then you're rushing through the pipes again. You gasp for breath.

SPLASH! The current lets you go. You're drifting in a big, broad, smelly river. You tread water and gaze around. The only light trickles in through tiny openings in the grates far overhead. Empty paper cups and bits of food float by you.

The whole river smells like rotten garbage. Slimy strings of filth wind around your arms and neck. Gross! You're in the sewer system!

You swim to one of the sides, but the banks are too steep and slimy to climb. You can't tread water for ever. Already your arms are getting tired.

Then something familiar floats by.

If it's a Popsicle stick, go to PAGE 52.
If it's a blue plastic can with the words MON-STER BLOOD on it, turn to PAGE 11.

"I've been looking for a great experiment," Dr Abbott exclaims. "I don't know anything about size change. But I'm willing to give it a shot."

"I'll try anything," you say. "I'm desperate."

"Excellent! Just think of the publicity!" Dr Abbott is getting very excited. "People will stop accusing me of—" He glances down at you. "Well, never mind. Let's get started."

The scientist hurries to his desk and searches through piles of papers. "I have to do a bit of research," he explains.

You smile weakly at him. You hope you haven't made a terrible mistake.

Finally, Dr Abbott lifts you up in his hand and examines you carefully. Every time he exhales, the force of his breath almost blows you over. He takes out a tape measure and measures you. He puts you on scales and weighs you. Then he places you on a table.

"I'm not sure which one of my machines to use," he says. "The magnetron works by changing your magnetic field. The laser gun makes the body's atoms expand. What do you think?"

"What do *I* think?" you reply with a gulp. Somehow, you hadn't expected the decision to be yours. Still, it *is* your body.

Do you want to try magnetism? Go to PAGE 76.

Or is the laser gun the answer? Turn to PAGE 101.

You take a step back, but the tiger bounds up to you. Its lips twist in a snarl and its teeth glisten in the bright lights.

"Aaaaaarrrggghh!" The piercing sound of your scream even shocks *you*. The tiger freezes mid-pounce. The crowd stares at you. You'd forgotten how loud your voice is, now that you are a giant.

The tiger backs away, and then, with its tail between its legs, skulks back to the ring.

"I'm sorry, kitty," you call to the frightened animal.

You didn't mean to scare it. And you realize that now that you are huge, the tigers couldn't really hurt you. As you stride to the centre of the ring, all the tigers cower. Even the trainer looks a little nervous. You reach out to the tiger and scratch it under its chin. Then it starts to rub against your legs like a kitten. It's purring!

The crowd begins applauding and cheering. But the tiger trainer just glares at you.

"Nice kitty," you tell the tiger. You kneel down and pet the beautiful animal. You notice the tiger trainer is still glaring at you. Oooops— it finally dawns on you—you've interrupted his performance. You'd better get out of the ring. You straighten back up and turn to go.

Yeowch! Something just yanked your hair— hard!

Go to PAGE 10.

There is an odd number of letters in your first name.

And you have a new idea for fighting the mouse.

You stop duelling with the rodent. Instead, you circle around a sauce pot. The mouse starts to follow you. You speed up.

And there it is! The mouse's tail. Quickly, you grab it and hold on.

The mouse squeaks in anger and begins to run through the cupboard. You continue to hold on to its tail.

Then, just as you hoped, the mouse runs towards the front of the cupboard. Its weight and its momentum should do the trick. Yes! When it hits the cupboard door, the door pops open.

Quickly, you let go of the mouse's tail. You run out of the cupboard and into the kitchen.

You turn around and see the mouse lying on the floor. It must have stunned itself when it hit the cupboard door. But it's starting to wake up.

There's only one thing to do.

What is it?

Turn to PAGE 116.

Barney's right.

You are a wimp.

This adventure is cancelled on account of nerdiness.

What?

You want another chance?

Okay.

You can stand up to Barney the Bully by rushing over to PAGE 26!

Dora is shrieking and staring at you in horror.

"Dora—" you say. "It's me, your cousin!"

But you're so big she doesn't even recognize you. And you can tell you're still growing.

"Help!" she screams. "Help! It's a mutant alien!"

You pull yourself to your feet. Maybe if she can see all of you she'll know who you are. As you stand, your hair brushes the treetops. Dora looks very small standing in the garden beneath you.

And now Barney runs out of the house.

"Call the police!" Dora screams. "There's a mutant alien in our back garden!"

Barney takes one look at you and turns white. He spins around and heads for the house.

He's going to call the police! They've already been called about you once. If they come again, you'll be in so much trouble you'll never get out of it. You've got to stop Barney. But how?

Grab him and try to explain? Turn to PAGE 6.

Or throw something in his path on PAGE 83.

"It's the alien!" A blond kid in row two points at you.

"I'm not an alien!" you shout. "I'm a human kid!"

More people begin screaming, "The alien! It's the alien!"

In shock, you drop the elephant. This makes the elephant furious. She swoops you up in her powerful trunk. At first you think she is going to squeeze you to death. Then Dodo lifts you into the air and swings you back and forth.

"Call the police!" someone shouts. Now the entire audience is shrieking. The situation is getting ugly. A dozen security guards start running towards you.

You thought you were safe here. But now everyone thinks you're an alien.

Then you spot your cousin Dora sitting right in the front row.

You've never been so happy to see her before in your whole life. In fact, this is probably the *only* time you've been happy to see her.

"Tell them, Dora!" you shout. "Save me! Tell them I'm not an alien!"

Dora stares back at you. Then she smiles.

Hooray! You're saved!

Turn to PAGE 65.

You refuse to be defeated. "I've got an idea," you tell Dr Abbott. "We'll make a staircase." You and Dr Abbott struggle and strain as you shove books into a pile. The books are stacked unevenly, forming steps. When the pile is as tall as the beaker, you and the scientist rush up the steps. At the top, you reach out for the remote. It's nearly as big as you are.

Your hands both touch the remote. With all your strength, you pull. You fall flat on your back. But the remote lands next to you.

"I'll change the settings!" Dr Abbott cries. He presses a button on the remote. The buttons are so big he has to use both hands. Then, grunting and sweating, he turns a dial.

"That should do it," he tells you. "On the count of three, jump on button number six. At the same time, I'll put all my weight on the 'on' switch. One!

"Two!"

You prepare to jump on to button six.

"Three!" Will you be successful? That depends on the month you were born in.

If you were born in the first half of the year— between January and June—turn to PAGE 30.

If you were born between the months of July and December, turn to PAGE 68.

Quickly, before your cousin can catch you up, you dart outside through the kitchen door. You may be small, but you're a fast runner.

You glance around for a good hiding-place. No time to be choosy. You dash on to the lawn, then duck under the porch.

The kitchen door slams again. Then you hear Barney's footsteps clomping over your head. You crouch while Barney stumbles around on the lawn, calling your name.

"I'll give you ten to come out!" he shouts.

You smile to yourself. How stupid can he be? Why should you come out and get beaten up when you can relax under here, safe and comfortable?

"One!" Barney cries. "Three! Seven!"

He's cheating again, but you don't care. You're safe, at least for now. And you can wait a lot longer than Barney can count.

Yup! Just as you expected, Barney gets bored and heads back into the house. You figure you'll give Barney plenty of time to cool off.

While you wait, you see those pink dots again. But other than that, it's pretty comfy under the porch.

After you think you've waited long enough, you start to crawl out from under the porch. Then you stop in horror.

Quick! Turn to PAGE 18.

It's your cousin Dora—smirking at you from the top of the stairs.

"You're not supposed to be down here," she whines. "I'm going to tell!"

"Wait!" you cry. "It was an accident! I came in here by mistake!"

"Yeah, sure," she taunts. "But maybe I won't tell—if you play with me."

"Maybe," you say cautiously.

"Let's play dolls," she urges. "I have a new doll's house."

You hate playing with Dora. She's really spoilt and has a tantrum if she doesn't get her way.

"I'll tell if you don't," Dora persists.

What are you going to do?

If you refuse to budge, turn to PAGE 22.

If you give in and play with Dora, turn to PAGE 35.

You try to think of any possible reason why you could suddenly start growing. You think back over everything you've done for the past twenty-four hours. You still haven't figured out an answer when you enter the kitchen.

Dora and Barney are making sandwiches in the kitchen. You are really hungry now. Along with everything else, your appetite has also grown. But when you reach for the tuna fish, Barney stops you. "You ought to go on a diet, wimp," he tells you. "You're getting fat—or haven't you noticed?"

Dora giggles obnoxiously.

You know perfectly well that you're not fat—you're just big. Big and hungry!

Then you remember something. You were very hungry when you were hiding in the basement. Hungry enough to eat that stale chocolate cake. Maybe there was some ingredient in the cake that is making you grow. It did taste kind of funny.

If you find out what was in the cake, you should be able to figure out how to stop growing!

Rush down to the basement on PAGE 34.

You don't stand up straight away. You feel a little woozy from the effects of the machine. You lie on the bench and gaze up at Arnold. He is staring at you, his eyes growing wider and wider.

Not a good sign.

"Uh, Arnold," you begin, "did it work?"

His mouth opens and closes, but he doesn't answer you.

Definitely not a good sign.

You leap off the bench. You run to a mirror and your heart nearly stops. You're back to your normal height. But your body has totally changed!

The flapping motion made your arms stretch. Your hands dangle below your knees! The swimming movement made your legs as thick as tree trunks. The helmet shrank your head to half its normal size!

"I'm afraid I got the setting wrong," Arnold says. "I should have read the instructions first."

Now he tells you!

THE END

You pick up the crumb of chocolate cake, place it in your mouth, and swallow. A moment later, you feel an electric tingling all over your body.

The next instant, you feel a sharp pain in your head.

Your head has hit the top of the refrigerator. You're growing big again! The chocolate cake worked!

You jump out of the refrigerator, rubbing your head. Then you grin while you watch all the junk around you in the dump appear to shrink.

In just a few seconds you've returned to normal kid-size.

You arrive back at your aunt's house in time for lunch. Barney is waiting for you on the porch.

"Where have you been, wimp?" he demands.

"Out," you say.

"Oh, yeah?" He pulls back his hand to give you a karate chop. But to his surprise, and yours too, you move quickly to block it.

"OW!" Barney whines, rubbing his hand. "How did you do that?"

You don't answer. You're not sure. But it seems the cake not only made you bigger, it made you faster and stronger. Maybe the rest of the summer won't be so bad after all.

THE END

You've decided to try to fight the mouse. It's heading straight towards you, and it looks mean! Mean and hungry.

But it's so big—you need a weapon. You glance around desperately.

You spot a box of utensils hanging on the inside of the cupboard door. Inside the box are some pins for holding corn on the cob. One end of each pin is sharp. The other end has a plastic handle. You grab one of the pins by the handle. It's as big as a sword to you.

Then you turn to face the mouse.

It approaches, baring its ugly yellow teeth. It lunges at you. You lunge back, holding your pin like a sword. The mouse easily dodges the pin.

It reaches out a clawed paw and rakes your arm. You cry out in pain and thrust back with the pin.

The two of you seem well matched. So well that the only way to determine the outcome of this duel between human and beast is by chance.

Count the number of letters in your first name.

If you have an EVEN number of letters, turn to PAGE 25.

If the number of letters is ODD, turn to PAGE 88.

You head for the metal pile as fast as you can run.

You hear the lizard coming after you. You race ahead, faster than you've ever run before.

The lizard's sticky tongue darts out of its mouth. It touches the back of your shirt. You break away. You reach the rusty metal. Now you realize it's a pile of wrecked cars.

You climb on to the crushed metal door of one of the cars. The lizard starts up after you. You climb through the window and leap on to the dashboard.

You glance at the window. The lizard glances back at you.

Where can you hide?

Then you spot the open glove compartment. Perfect! You crawl in and slam the door behind you.

There's no way the lizard can get in. You glance around. The glove compartment is full of old, torn maps. There's a rusty torch, a bunch of keys, and a half-eaten roll of mints. To you, they're all the size of furniture.

You lean against a map and relax. But then you hear a deafening roar. The car starts to tilt. Then it begins to shake.

Quick! Turn to PAGE 114.

100

It's gone! The refrigerator has disappeared.

In fact, all the furniture in the basement has gone! Everything. The basement is completely empty!

You rush to the kitchen. Your aunt is just leaving the house to go to work at the university.

"Aunt Fiona!" you cry. "Where's the refrigerator that was in the basement?"

She frowns. "Dora told me you were playing down there yesterday," she replies.

That rat! You played with her stupid doll's house and she still told on you.

"Don't worry," Aunt Fiona goes on. "I had all the furniture hauled to the dump early this morning."

"But—" you start to protest.

"Those old things were dirty and dangerous," she continues. "Now it's safe for you kids to play down there whenever you want." She gives you a quick kiss and leaves before you can ask any more questions.

You stare after her in shock. You're in big trouble. Or, rather, in small trouble. You're still shrinking. What if you grow so small you disappear?

If you think you can find the refrigerator at the dump, hurry to PAGE 24.

If you think you should see a doctor, turn to PAGE 120.

"I'd like to try the laser treatment," you squeak.

"Excellent!" Dr Abbott replies. "Now stay right there."

He rushes across the room and returns pushing a huge machine. It looks like a white machine-gun with a pointed barrel. He aims it directly at you.

Dr Abbott presses several buttons on a plastic remote control. With a high-pitched whine, the laser starts up. Suddenly, a red ray shoots out. You start to sweat and pant. But you're not growing any bigger.

Dr Abbott turns off the machine. "Any results?" he asks.

"It isn't working," you tell him.

"Oh, dear," he says, frowning. "Maybe I'd better turn the ray up to full power." He presses more buttons on the remote. There's a sudden *POP!* and the entire room glows bright red.

You fall down as everything begins to shake. The red light is so bright you have to cover your eyes. Then it begins to fade to pink. The shaking stops and the laser shuts off.

You're still small.

And Dr Abbott seems to have disappeared.

"Dr Abbott?" you call. "Dr Abbott?" You approach the edge of the table and glance down. There on the floor is a tiny creature wearing a white lab coat. It looks like . . .

Quick! Turn to PAGE 36!

102

"What's wrong?" you ask Dora.

"Why is your watch like that?" she asks, pointing to your wrist.

You glance where Dora is pointing and notice that your wristwatch is hanging loose from your wrist. "That's strange," you murmur. "The watchband must have stretched."

"It's metal," Dora points out. "How could it stretch? Didn't it fit when you got here?"

"I think so," you mumble.

That's a good question, you realize, but one you don't have an answer for.

Now you notice something else. When you first came here, you were seven centimetres taller than Dora. Sitting beside her now, you seem to be the same height. How could that be possible?

What is going on? Rush to PAGE 78.

You rush out of the house and turn right. But you have to stop for a minute. Pink spots appear before your eyes and your toes tingle. Once the weird feeling passes, you run down the street towards the number 103 bus stop.

When you hurry by your uncle's mailbox, you see it's now higher than your head. You've shrunk even more!

Just as you arrive at the bus stop, the 103 bus pulls up. You start to hop on board.

"Just a minute," says the bus driver. "How old are you?"

"I'm twelve," you reply.

The driver laughs. "Nice try. But no twelve-year-old could be so small. I'm afraid you're too young to ride on the bus by yourself. Come back with one of your parents."

"But I have to go to the university!" you protest.

"Sorry," the bus driver says. "Rules are rules." He shuts the door in your face. Too bad. It looks as if you made the wrong choice. And this adventure is over.

But wait! You have one more chance. You can still try to track down the refrigerator and see if the jar of purple peanut butter is inside. Hurry back to your uncle's house. That will be a safe place to come up with a plan!

Turn to PAGE 58.

104

You've heard that water bugs sometimes fly, but you've never seen one do it.

And you hope you never will again.

For now, though, you realize you are lucky you found one that can. This is your chance to get out of the sewer.

But first, you've got to figure out some way to steer before you slide off the bug's slimy back. You grasp the left antenna and pull hard. The water bug turns left. You pull on the right antenna, and it turns right. The antennae work just like reins!

You steer the water bug along the sewer until you reach an overhead storm drain. You guide the insect up through the drain and out into the street.

Then you kick the bug in the sides. It begins to fly high, higher. Soon the town is far below. You scan the countryside. And then you see it— the Fiskeville dump.

You guide the water bug south towards the dump. The dump is huge. It stretches over several acres. How will you find the refrigerator?

The insect begins to fly faster as it approaches the dump. It dips low and skims a metre or so above the dump. It's heading straight for a big mound of rotting garbage!

Quick! Jump off the water bug and turn to PAGE 59.

You'll try the steam room. You don't want to test out some new contraption.

Arnold gives you a large bathing-suit to change into. Then you step through a door into a room that's filled with billowing clouds of steam.

It's HOT in here! The steam fills your eyes, your mouth, your nose. You begin to sweat. You sit on a wooden bench. The steam grows hotter. You sweat even more. You feel the bathing-suit growing loose on your body.

It's working! You're shrinking!

The warm steam makes all your muscles relax. You feel as if you don't have a care in the world. You get sleepy . . . sleepy.

You wake up incredibly thirsty. Water, you think, you have to get some water. Your legs feel rubbery when you slide off the bench. You stumble to the door and try to open it.

You can't reach the handle.

The steam worked too well. You've shrunk—just like your sweater when you accidentally put it in the hot-water wash.

"Let me out!" you cry, pounding on the door.

You realize that Arnold has forgotten all about you.

The steam continues to pour in. You continue to shrink. When you have shrunk down to the size of a raisin you give up hope.

This steamy adventure has come to a sweltering

END

106

You turn around and start for the highway.

You have to be very careful where you put your feet—whoops! There went someone's bicycle. *CRUNCH!* You've just flattened Uncle Harvey's car!

You hope you don't accidentally crush a person or animal.

You step carefully over a parked van. The neighbourhood still rings with terrified shouts: "ALIEN! ALIEN!"

You can't wait to get away!

Once you reach the main road, you take off. *CRASH!* Cars collide behind you—but you have to keep going. You don't even dare look back. Then you hear a frightening sound: sirens.

Lots of sirens.

Someone in your uncle's neighbourhood has called the police. You are in big trouble now. And if your neighbours won't listen to you, will the police?

You see flashing lights in the distance as the emergency vehicles race towards you. Above them helicopters buzz like angry hornets.

It's an all-out attack! Where can you go? What can you do?

And then you see it—one of the few places in the world where you might be able to hide until you return to your normal size.

Turn to PAGE 54.

You bend down and lick up the smear of icing. Then you wait.

At first nothing happens.

Then your arms start to ache and your mouth feels strange. Something is happening to you! You watch as the refrigerator appears to grow smaller.

You're growing! It's working!

You hop out of the refrigerator. As you do, the lizard hops *in* the refrigerator. It climbs up to the cake box and gobbles up the crumb of cake.

You turn to head back for your uncle's house.

Then you hear a *CRASH* behind you. You glance back to see that the lizard completely fills the refrigerator. The crumb made it grow, too!

Turn to PAGE 55.

108

"One," Barney counts. "Two, three, four, twenty-seven, twenty-eight, fifty . . ."

As usual, your cousin is cheating. You'll have to find a place to hide, fast.

But where? Dora drops Puff and runs around to the back of the house. You want to stay as far away from her as possible. You glance around, then tiptoe into the house.

You find yourself in a small living room crowded with furniture. You don't have much time. Where can you hide?

You dodge around a couple of chairs. Then you head for a hallway that leads to the kitchen.

"Seventy!" Barney shouts from outside. "Eight-one! Eighty-six!"

You spot a doorway to the right of the refrigerator. You pull the door open. Steep, splintery steps lead down into a dark, musty-smelling room. It must be the way to the basement.

But your aunt and uncle warned you to stay out of it.

"Ninety-three!" Barney shouts.

Quick! Make a decision. Should you forget about your aunt and uncle's warning and hide in the basement? Or find somewhere else to hide?

To creep down to the basement, turn to PAGE 71.

Or find another hiding-place on PAGE 47.

You run down the hall as fast as your tiny legs can go. The caretaker's footsteps thunder behind you.

You duck into Dr Abbott's lab at the end of the hall. You hide in the space between the open door and the wall.

"Where's that mouse?" the caretaker shouts.

"There are no mice in here," says a friendly voice from the back of the room. You glance up to see a tall scientist with a grey beard working at a table. He must be Dr Abbott, you think.

"Let's look around to make sure," the caretaker insists. You hold your breath as he enters the room, then clomps around looking for you.

Please don't look behind the door, you think.

"I guess it didn't come in here," the caretaker announces. "See you later, Doc."

You let out a sigh of relief. You step out from behind the door and glance around. Dr Abbott's laboratory is huge. Way above your head you can see several tables and bookshelves. Two big metal machines stand in a corner. You hear the sound of something boiling on a gas burner.

You're sure to find help here. But how can you make Dr Abbott notice you?

Turn to PAGE 9.

110

The eyes are in the middle of an orange, furry face. It looks just like a giant tiger! The beast licks its lips.

You realize it's not really a tiger, but it might as well be. It's Dora's cat, Puff. It doesn't know you're a human. All it knows is that you look a lot like dinner.

"Nice kitty," you say, backing slowly towards the porch steps. "Nice Puff, nice, nice."

The cat blinks once, then crouches low to the ground. The cat is about to pounce.

You sprint to the steps. You have to stand on your tiptoes to reach the first one. You strain to pull yourself up by your hands. It's like climbing up the side of a building.

You hear Puff, behind you, growling softly.

The next step is much easier to climb. It's weathered, and you use splinters as handholds.

The last step is also covered with splinters. They catch on your clothes and poke your skin. You climb up as quickly as you can. You reach the porch, exhausted. But you can't rest.

Puff is preparing to spring straight towards you.

The screen door is open a couple of centimetres. But it's all the way across the porch. Do you have time to make it there?

Or should you head for Dora's doll's house a metre or so away?

Run for the door on PAGE 19.
Or head for the doll's house, PAGE 44.

You decide to taste the cake. That purple peanut butter looks too weird. You are so hungry, your mouth waters when you take a big bite of the cake.

The frosting is hard, the cake is crumbly, and there is a funny aftertaste. You've definitely had better.

But chocolate is chocolate. Besides, you're starving! Your mouth is open for another bite when you hear your aunt calling your name.

Uh-oh! Your aunt's still at home. You don't want to get caught in the basement! What can you do? Your eyes dart around the basement, searching for a way out.

The basement window! You hurry across the room and scramble on to the back of the sofa. By standing on your tiptoes, you can just reach the grimy window-sill. You hoist yourself up.

Luckily, the window is open. You slither through, flopping on to the grass.

Great! No one will ever know you were in the basement. Problem solved.

But then you roll over on to your back.

And face a new problem.

What is it? Turn to PAGE 27.

112

You glance down the street. A police car is speeding towards the park. Its red lights blink and its siren wails.

"You're in big trouble now!" Barney calls. Without looking back, he dashes away. Thanks a lot, cousin, you think. He disappears into the distance.

"It wasn't your fault," the red-haired pitcher says. "It was just a great hit."

"You'd better get out of here fast," another player suggests.

You don't know what to do. You didn't mean to break the window. But will the police believe you? What will they do? Maybe you'd better hide until they go away.

If you wait for the police and confess, turn to PAGE 73.

If you run and hide, race to PAGE 4.

"I'd love to join the circus," you tell the clown.

"Great!" he exclaims. "We'll work out the details later. You'll work with the tigers. Starting now!"

As the audience files in for the next show, Tombo, the tiger trainer, gives you a nasty look. "You don't know anything about tigers, kid," Tombo warns. "They can be very dangerous. And people can be dangerous, too!"

Is he threatening you? Before you can find out, the ringmaster announces your act: "And now presenting Tombo the Tiger Trainer and his amazing new assistant!"

The circus band strikes up a song. The spotlight focuses on the centre ring. Tombo lets his five tigers out of the cage. The big cats jump on to their stands inside the ring.

They snarl and growl as Tombo approaches. Tombo holds up a flaming hoop. He cracks his whip. One by one, he makes the tigers jump through the flames. The crowd applauds. "Let's see you top *that*, kid," he sneers.

You feel sorry for the tigers. They may be dangerous animals, but you can tell they don't like the whip or jumping through hoops. But somehow, you have to entertain the crowd.

"Go on, kid!" Tombo whispers. "Get started! If you want to keep your job!"

Get to work on PAGE 56.

The car shakes even harder. Is this an earthquake?

You open the glove compartment part way. The lizard has gone. But—oh, no!

You glance up through the car window. The car is caught in a gigantic machine. The machine is pushing the car towards the huge steel jaws of a car crusher!

You've got to get out of here!

You jump out of the glove compartment. You race across the seat. *If you can just make it back out of the window* . . . But the vibrations throw you to the floor.

You scramble up again. Maybe there's a hole in the floor! Or maybe you can get the car door open! You hurl yourself against the car door. It doesn't budge.

The sound of the car crusher is deafening. With a jolt, you are thrown off your feet again. As you peer up from the floor, you see that the roof of the car is coming closer.

And closer.

And closer.

In another few seconds, the car crusher will mash the car—and you—into a metal pancake.

Alas, for you, this adventure has come to a SMASHING

END

That floor is a long way down.

You decide it would be safer to climb down and then back up the other table. It may take a bit longer, but at least you'll get there in one piece.

You work your way down the table leg. Luckily, the table leg has carvings that give you good places to put your feet.

Once you make it to the floor, you scurry over to the lab table. You peer up and see that Dr Abbott is more than halfway to the top.

"I'm right behind you," you call up to him. You quickly begin your climb. You pull yourself up, hand over hand. It's tough going, but you are making progress. You glance up again. Dr Abbott is just pulling himself up on to the top of the table.

Unfortunately, he grabs on to the corner of a huge encyclopaedia. The enormous volume tips over the edge of the table. Dr Abbott manages to swing his legs up and scrambles out of the way.

You're not so lucky.

"Oh, no!" you squeak. The book tumbles off the table, knocking you from the table leg. You land on the floor with a bone-shattering thud. A pile of books crashes on top of you.

Too bad.

What's the scientific term for SQUASHED?

THE END

116

You've decided to make friends with the mouse. You want it to know you aren't a threat.

"Hello, mousey, mousey," you say sweetly. You try not to think about its long, yellow teeth.

The mouse stops stalking you. It stares at you with its little beady eyes. You think back on all the mice you've seen in school science projects. You know they're curious animals. How can you make it curious—instead of hungry?

You begin to make faces at it. You rub your stomach with one hand while patting your head with the other. The mouse continues to gaze at you. It seems much less dangerous now. It starts to appear interested.

Now you do a cartwheel. When you're upside down, you hit your heel on a pot lid.

"Ow!" you cry. The mouse squeaks at you, as if it understands that you hurt yourself.

You make squeaking sounds back at the mouse. Maybe you can convince it that you're just a strange-looking mouse.

"SQUEAK!" the mouse cries.

"SCREEK!" you reply.

And then, suddenly, the mouse lunges at you. Its mouth is wide open. Have you made a mistake? Did you say something terrible in mouse squeaks?

Turn to PAGE 45.

It's a sound you never thought you'd be happy to hear—the voice of your cousin. "Puff!" Dora cries. "What are you doing by the doll's house?"

You hear a creaking noise and light floods the kitchen. Dora pulls the roof off the doll's house. "See?" she tells Puff. "There's nothing in here, it's—what's that?"

Now you see her round eyes staring in at you.

"Why, it looks like a little person!" she exclaims, reaching for you.

"I'm your cousin!" you shout. "Don't you recognize me?"

But your voice is a pathetic squeak. There's no way she can hear you. "Cool!" she murmurs. "Another doll to play with!"

"But I'm not a doll!" you protest.

"Stay right here," Dora goes on. "I'll go and get some goodies for you to eat. We can play tea party. Won't it be fun?"

"Wait!" you cry. But before you can protest again, she replaces the lid on the doll's house. All you can do now is wait for her to return. Maybe you'll be able to talk some sense into her. Or maybe not.

If only Puff would go away.

And then you hear another voice. From *inside* the doll's house.

Turn to PAGE 82.

118

You can't join the circus! You have to find a way to make yourself smaller. "Thanks for your offer," you tell the clown. "But I'm not usually this big." You explain your problem.

"I understand," the clown tells you. "I appreciate your honesty. In return, I may be able to help you. One of our workers is a fortune-teller who has strange powers. She may be able to return you to your normal size."

After the show, the clown introduces you to a very small white-haired woman in a long pink robe. Her face is so wrinkled she appears to be hundreds of years old.

"I predict," she begins in a strange accent, "you will make lots of money and live a long, happy life."

"No, no," the clown says. "We don't need a fortune told. This person needs help!"

"That's different," she says. "My fortunes are all fake." You notice her accent has now disappeared.

Your heart sinks. You thought she was going to be someone with real powers.

"But my powers are very real," she says, as if she had read your mind. "But I don't use them on fortunes. Everyone wants the same thing. Fame, money, success . . ." She sighs. "Now, tell me—what's your problem?"

Tell her on PAGE 7.

"What's the condition?" Barney sobs. "I'll do anything you say. Anything at all."

"First," you say, "you have to promise not to call the police."

"I promise," Barney cries.

"You must also promise that from now on you'll be nice to your cousin. You'll share your bike and all your toys. And you'll never pound anyone ever again."

"I promise," Barney gulps.

"Very well," you announce. "You may live."

You prepare to set him down when your whole body suddenly begins to feel warm. It feels almost as if—

Uh-oh.

What's happening? Find out on PAGE 46.

You decide the best thing to do is see a doctor.

But how will you find one? You check by the phone. That's where parents usually keep emergency phone numbers. And this is definitely an emergency.

You're in luck! There's a list posted on the wall. And right between the phone number for the police and the phone number for pizza delivery, there's a number for a Dr Jenner.

You dial quickly. You try not to notice how far you have to stretch to reach the phone.

A woman's voice comes on the line. "Dr Jenner's office."

"I have to see the doctor immediately," you say.

"What's the problem?" the woman asks.

"I'm shrinking!" you blurt out.

There's dead silence on the other end of the line.

"Please! You have to help me," you beg. "My clothes are too big, I can't reach the phone, and my watch—"

"May I speak to an adult?" the woman breaks in.

You can tell she doesn't believe you. "No one is home," you explain. "And this is an emergency."

"The doctor is very busy," the woman says coldly. "And I don't have time for prank phone calls."

You slam down the phone in frustration.

Now what? Turn to PAGE 12.

The police are still after you. And they've sent for reinforcements. You head away from the circus, towards the highway.

The sirens are growing closer. Your heart pounds in terror as you see blinking emergency lights approaching on the highway. How will you ever get out of here?

You glance in the other direction. More lights. More sirens.

And an elephant!

"AROOOOO!" Dodo trumpets. She must have followed you.

You glance at the elephant. She definitely likes you. She actually seems to be smiling.

You stare back at the highway. Then you get an idea.

"Dodo," you whisper, "how would you like to do me a really big favour?"

"AROOOO!" the elephant answers. It's as if Dodo understands you.

"Dodo," you tell the elephant. "Here's the plan. You distract them while I run away."

You could swear Dodo nods at you. You pat Dodo on the rear. The elephant lumbers down the highway. Right towards the police.

You watch as the police cars skid and swerve to avoid the elephant. Dodo swings her trunk at the cars. She seems to be having a good time.

You take off in the opposite direction.

Run to PAGE 41.

122

Dora reaches into the box and pulls out Aunt Fiona's eye make-up. Then she leans closer to the mirror.

You jump up and grab a large bath towel that's dangling from the towel rack next to the sink. You begin to climb it, using the rough threads for handholds.

You've nearly reached the sink when the towel starts to slip. Your weight is pulling it down!

Your only choice is to leap on to the sink. You barely make it. You hang on to the slippery porcelain by your fingertips. Then you pull yourself all the way on to the sink.

All this time Dora continues to put on make-up. Badly. She's now applying mascara. "Dora!" you yell.

She picks up a tube and pulls off the top. Then she starts to put on lipstick. She's smearing it all over her face.

"Dora!" you repeat. You try to get right under her and nearly trip over a toothbrush. As you regain your balance, one of your feet slides out from under you. You're skidding on a smear of toothpaste on the porcelain. Somehow, you keep from sliding off the edge of the sink.

Dora is still gazing at herself in the mirror.

This isn't working. You've got to do something more obvious.

Get noticed on PAGE 70.

"I'll never surrender!" you reply. You turn to run.

"Capture the alien!" Dr Harlan shouts. "Don't let it get away!"

You wish! you think. How can they catch you? You're twenty times as big as any of them.

But on the other hand, where can you go?

Do you really want to spend the rest of your life trying to escape? Maybe if you talk to Dr Harlan, you can convince him you're not an alien. Maybe he can use his scientific knowledge to return you to your normal size.

You stop running and turn back. Dr Harlan's red van is heading straight for you.

"I want to talk," you announce.

The van stops. Dr Harlan steps out. "I'm listening!" he calls. "You have thirty seconds to explain yourself."

You think carefully. Whatever you say next could affect your whole future. But before you can begin, you suddenly feel very strange. You're dizzy, and your mouth has become dry. Painfully dry.

What's going on?

Find out on PAGE 20.

You wait for Puff to lift her paw. Then you dash for the door as fast as you can.

But Puff is too quick for you. With amazing force, she smashes you with her paw. You fly across the porch. Everything goes black.

When you come to, you are in bed. Aunt Fiona must have found you and brought you upstairs, you think.

Then you realize something—something wonderful! The bed is the right size! The pillow fits your head perfectly! You pull up the blankets, and your toes pop out the other end. You're back to normal! You are your normal size again.

You feel great. You leap to your feet and run over to inspect yourself in the mirror. It's hanging at the perfect height. You don't even have to stand on your toes to see your reflection. Maybe it was all just a bad dream, you think.

But then you notice something terrifying outside the window. It's a pair of giant yellow eyes, gazing down at you. Gigantic eyes in a huge tiger face.

Puff!

Somehow, you ended up in the doll's house. No wonder the miniature furniture was just the right size for you.

You are a miniature kid.

Sorry. I guess this wasn't your lucky day after all.

THE END

You lick up *all* the powder on your palm.

A second later, your mouth feels as if it's on fire! This is the hottest stuff you've ever tasted!

You rush outside the big top searching for water. You spot a big tank that's used to water the animals. You grab it up and drain it in one gulp!

It doesn't help. You've got to find more water!

You rush away from the circus. In the distance you see a lake. You take three big steps, and you're there. You kneel down and begin to sip from the lake.

By the time the lake is empty, you start to feel better. You stand up—and notice that you're bigger. Much, much bigger.

You're so big that the dry lake is a tiny dot far below you.

A jet plane buzzes by your ear.

You're so big your feet cover a whole county!

It appears that you took too much of the herbal powder. It's having a reverse effect!

Uh-oh! You can't breathe. You're so tall your head reaches into outer space.

Too bad, it looks as if this big adventure was really out of this world!

THE END

126

Better stick to your original plan. Your aunt will definitely want to help you. These scientists might want to turn you into an experiment!

You hurry towards the main building, but you aren't getting very far. Since your feet are now the size of a normal human's fingernail, it's no surprise.

You're exhausted. But you finally spot the administration building. Just as you take a step, those pink dots swim in front of your eyes. That awful tingling starts again.

When everything returns to normal you are shocked by how tiny you are. A blade of grass seems as big as an oak tree!

Then, the dots appear again! Oh, no! You're still shrinking!

You took too long to get help. And now, it's too late. You are shrinking down to nothing.

Going, going,

THE END

You watch as the huge beast climbs through the hole towards you. Its face is covered with hair. It has a long, pointed snout and huge yellow teeth. It opens its mouth and lets out a loud *SQUEAK!*

You realize that the terrifying monster is a mouse!

And it's three times bigger than you are.

You are really small now!

The mouse glances around the cupboard, probably looking for food. Then it spots you.

Its long whiskers twitch as it sniffs in your direction. It begins to move towards you.

What will you do now? Should you try to fight it off?

Or maybe it's as gentle as the mice in the cage in your school classroom. Maybe you should make friends with it.

Whatever you decide, you've got to do something soon! There's no way out of the cupboard except through the mouse hole. And the mouse is now less than a whisker away!

Fight the mouse? Turn to PAGE 98.
Or make friends with it? Try PAGE 116.

128

The dinosaur's long, grey body is covered with scales. It grips the ground with cruel-looking claws. Its narrow tongue flicks in and out of its wide mouth.

But it can't possibly be here! Dinosaurs became extinct millions of years ago.

Then you realize that it's not a dinosaur. It's a grey, striped lizard. But you're so small now, it might as well be Tyrannosaurus rex!

The lizard fixes its beady eyes on you. It flicks its tongue out again. Then it begins marching towards you.

It thinks you're its dinner!

Quick! Get out of here now!

Head for the pile of twisted metal on PAGE 99.

Or run for the jungle—PAGE 60.

"I know you were down there," Dora continues in her whiny voice. "And if you won't play tea party with me, I'll tell."

Great, you think, I've been here less than a day, and I'm going to get into trouble already. Dora is such a pain.

"I don't want to play tea party!" you shout. Wow, you think, was that me? You can't believe how loud your voice has become.

Dora's eyes grow big. She actually looks afraid.

"You'd better not squeal on me," you command.

"Okay," Dora says. "I won't tell anybody you were in the basement." She hurries down the hall.

Getting bigger is great, you decide. Anything that makes both Barney *and* Dora stop bothering you is fantastic. This growth spurt happened at just the right time!

Now that you've got your cousins off your back, you decide to explore the neighbourhood. As you leave the house you realize that Uncle Harvey's shoes fit really well. Too well. They aren't big any more. Weird, you think. You must still be growing. You push the thought out of your mind.

You notice some kids playing baseball in an empty field across the street. You jog over to them.

Then you hear, "Get out of there, shrimp!" Barney is glaring at you from centre field.

If you stand up to Barney and join the game, turn to PAGE 26.

If you try to avoid him, turn to PAGE 89.

130

In front of the sideshow tent is a big sign: SEE THE BEARDED LADY. MEET THE MONKEY-FACED MAN. THRILLS AND CHILLS!

Quickly, you duck inside. You are amazed by what you see. Over in the corner a man covered from head to toe in tattoos is swallowing swords. A tiny woman and man in elegant clothes are watching his performance. They barely come up to the tattooed man's knees.

You glance to the opposite side of the tent. The fattest lady you have ever seen is trimming her long black beard. A man is helping her by holding a mirror. But he's standing on his hands and holding the mirror between his feet!

Hey, you think, being big isn't so bad here!

Just then, you feel something poke you in the shoulder. Startled, you turn and come face-to-face with a small, fat man in a yellow clown suit.

"You're late!" he scolds you. He sounds mad, but you can't help laughing. It's hard to take him too seriously with his white-face make-up and a giant painted red mouth.

"This is no laughing matter," he says. "It's show time! Now, get out there!" Before you can protest, he pokes you with a large tent pole.

"Youch!" you exclaim as you stumble through a flap in the curtain. It's dark. Something smells really gross. Where are you?

Find out on PAGE 84.

This magnetism might not be so bad, you think. Maybe this summer won't be so boring after all!

As you walk along the street, you pretend you are a magnetic superhero. Every time you pass by a metal pole, you act as if you are commanding it to bow down to you.

If only Barney and Dora were metal robots, you think. I'd have it made!

You think about how you can take advantage of your new magnetic power. Suddenly, you hear a strange sound. It almost sounds like a roaring ocean. You turn to see what could be making such a racket.

You can't believe what you are seeing! Hundreds and hundreds of cans are flying in your direction. They look like a swarm of giant metal bees. They soar over a high cement wall, heading straight for you. You glance at the sign on the wall.

FISKEVILLE RECYCLING CENTRE.

You are about to be crushed under thousands of pounds of recyclable cans—thanks to your magnetic personality.

THE END

132

You gaze at the kid in shock. The kid stares back, looking just as stunned. You realize what must have happened.

"The laser switched our bodies!" Dr Abbott cries. But he says it in *your* voice.

"I know," you reply, sounding like Dr Abbott.

"We have to switch back!" he exclaims.

You think for a moment. "Not yet," you reply.

"What do you mean, 'Not yet'?" Dr Abbott demands. "When?"

"After the summer is over," you say. *When I won't be stuck with Barney the Bully and Dull Dora any more*, you think.

"Out of the question!" Dr Abbott roars.

"Can you change back without my help?"

"Of course not!" Dr Abbott exclaims.

"Then I guess you don't have a choice," you state calmly. You go to the desk and find your aunt's number in the directory.

"What are you doing?" Dr Abbott demands as you punch in your aunt's number. "You can't just leave me like this!"

You hear Aunt Fiona's voice come on the line.

"Can you please get this kid out of here?" you bark in Dr Abbott's grown-up voice. "I can't get any work done!"

"Don't worry, Doc," you say as you hang up. "I'll come and get you as soon as I discover a formula to make my creepy cousins disappear."

THE END

The safety pin clatters to the ground.

You missed.

Well, you'll just have to try again.

You plant your feet, twirl the rope over your head, focus on the shelf and . . .

This time it works! The pin catches on the top shelf. With all your strength, you pull yourself hand over hand up the string.

By the time you're halfway up, your arm muscles are trembling. A breeze causes the string to swing out and away from the refrigerator. You swing back and forth. Back and forth. You hold on to the string tightly till the breeze dies down. Then you continue climbing.

At last you reach the top shelf. You let go of your rope-string and gaze around. Oh, no!

The jar has gone! All that's left is the chocolate-cake box.

Now what do you do? This was your last chance.

Go to PAGE 49.

134

What is happening to me? you wonder. Am I sick? Do I have a weird disease? If I keep getting bigger, I'm not going to fit into any of my clothes!

You stop in the middle of the street.

A terrible thought has just occurred to you.

What if you *never* stop growing?

You stand there, worrying, and a bus pulls up to the kerb and stops. You notice a huge advertisement plastered on its side:

GETTING TOO BIG?

CLOTHES SEEM TO BE SHRINKING?

THE SOLUTION IS AT ARNOLD'S!

Who is Arnold? you wonder. And could Arnold's be the answer to your problem?

If you go to Arnold's, turn to PAGE 61.
If you think you should continue home, go to PAGE 95.

You hear the sharp *CRACK!* as the bat connects with the ball. Then you watch, amazed, as the ball takes off, high in the air, clear across the field.

"Home run!" some of the kids shout.

You notice Barney's mouth drop open.

You don't move from the plate. You stare as the ball continues straight towards a house on the next block. You watch in disbelief as the ball smashes right through the enormous front window.

You don't even care that you broke the window. This was your first home run ever! As you round the bases your team-mates cheer. Even Barney looks impressed.

You feel great! Until you hear the unmistakable sound of police sirens.

Heading your way.

Go on to PAGE 112.

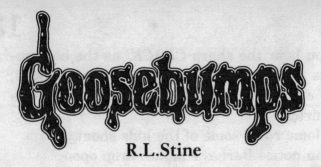

R.L.Stine

Reader beware, you're in for a scare!
These terrifying tales will send shivers up your spine:

Goosebumps

HIPPO GHOST

Secrets from the past... Danger in the present... Hippo Ghost brings you the spookiest of tales...

Summer Visitors
Emma thinks she's in for a really boring summer, until she meets the Carstairs family on the beach. But there's something very *strange* about her new friends...
Carol Barton

Ghostly Music
Beth loves her piano lessons. So why have they started to make her *ill...?*
Richard Brown

A Patchwork of Ghosts
Who is the evil-looking ghost tormenting Lizzie, and why does he want to hurt her...?
Angela Bull

The Ghosts who Waited
Everything's changed since Rosy and her family moved house. Why has everyone suddenly turned against her...?
Dennis Hamley

The Railway Phantoms

Rachel has visions. She dreams of two children in strange, disintegrating clothes. And it seems as if they are trying to contact her...

Dennis Hamley

The Haunting of Gull Cottage

Unless Kezzie and James can find what really happened in Gull Cottage that terrible night many years ago, the haunting may never stop...

Tessa Krailing

The Hidden Tomb

Can Kate unlock the mystery of the curse on Middleton Hall, before it destroys the Mason family...?

Jenny Oldfield

The House at the End of Ferry Road

The house at the end of Ferry Road has just been built. So it can't be haunted, can it...?

Martin Oliver

Beware! This House is Haunted
This House is Haunted Too!

Jessica doesn't believe in ghosts. So who *is* writing the strange, spooky messages?

Lance Salway

The Children Next Door

Laura longs to make friends with the children next door. But they're not quite what they seem...

Jean Ure

Goosebumps

Reader beware – here's THREE TIMES the scare!

Look out for these bumper GOOSEBUMPS editions. With three spine-tingling stories by R.L. Stine in each book, get ready for three times the thrill … three times the scare … three times the GOOSEBUMPS!

COLLECTION 1
Welcome to Dead House
Say Cheese and Die
Stay Out of the Basement

COLLECTION 2
The Curse of the Mummy's Tomb
Let's Get Invisible!
Night of the Living Dummy

COLLECTION 3
The Girl Who Cried Monster
Welcome to Camp Nightmare
The Ghost Next Door

COLLECTION 4
The Haunted Mask
Piano Lessons Can Be Murder
Be Careful What You Wish For

COLLECTION 5
The Werewolf of Fever Swamp
You Can't Scare Me!
One Day at HorrorLand

COLLECTION 6
Why I'm Afraid of Bees
Deep Trouble
Go Eat Worms

COLLECTION 7
Return of the Mummy
The Scarecrow Walks at Midnight
Attack of the Mutant